A Window Facing West

A Window Facing West

a novel

John S. Tarlton

Bridge Works Publishing Company
Bridgehampton, New York

Published in the United States by Bridge Works Publishing Company,
Bridgehampton, New York.
Distributed in the United States by National Book Network,
Lanham, Maryland.

First Edition

Library of Congress Cataloguing-in-Publication Data

Tarlton, John S., 1950–
A window facing west : a novel / John S. Tarlton.
p.   cm.
ISBN 1-882593-30-8 (hardcover : alk. paper)
I. Title.
PS3670.A833W56   1999
813'.54—dc 21   99-22549
                          CIP

This book is for Nancy

The author wishes to thank Ed Ruzicka, Charles deGravelles and Mary Louise Von Brock for their creative and editorial skills. The author is also grateful to Caroline Francis Carney of *Book Deals, Inc.;* she gave aid to a passing stranger. Profound thanks to Barbara A. Phillips and Claire Watson who gave the book its life.

"Come on, shake off the covers of this sloth,"
The master said, "for sitting softly cushioned,
Or tucked in bed, is no way to win fame;
And without it man must waste his life away,
leaving such traces of what he was on earth
as smoke in wind and foam upon the water.
Stand up! Dominate this weariness of yours . . ."

Dante: *The Divine Comedy*,
"Inferno", Canto XXIV

Part I

Wednesday, June 6

Midmorning

Chapter 1

Today is my forty-seventh birthday. Over breakfast, my blue-eyed spouse declares her summer vacation plans might not include a husband. Two friends of mine may be sleeping with the same mysterious woman. Packs of rabid beasts are roaming free. My father's ghost abides.

And it's not even eleven o'clock.

Here's the meat and potatoes: If it's just the sex thing lagging between my wife and me, maybe we can jump-start it. Sit down together over a tall drink like two rational adults and hash things out. Get some relief. Get Sarah, in all her hearty, cake-scented loveliness, to lie with me more often. Let me see the look of her yearning. Let me see.

The difficulty, after all, is neither the quality, intensity nor culmination of our lovemaking but rather of its frequency. Our ten-year-old cat has sex more often than we do. Somewhere along the line we allowed the incidence of our sex life to become a stratagem in the ongoing repartee. We punish each other with fussy abstinence. Sarah seems perfectly content with the once-a-week or so, winner-take-all, sexual catharsis we go through. For her making love is like going over the falls in a wooden barrel — sudden, astonishing, delirious — something you might care to do once or twice each summer but no more. Familiarity would take all the fun out of it.

Deep down below the floor of my belly, up against the white-hard bone of my spine, lurks a hunger that has little to do with orgasm. It is the unslakable lust for possession, for hot-blooded ardor and tactile ecstasy, for physical union — the plunging, entwined essence of man and woman joined, made one, with all the sundry differences between them nixed, obliterated, left behind.

What I'm alluding to is a mode of consciousness — the sublime state of *mutual being,* however brief or ineffable, a prolonged stirring of the pudding versus its hasty consumption. It's either that or become consumed by with my retirement planning.

Or, to step back and take the long view, is this not but another perfect illustration of God's fanciful, ribald sense of humor? Think about it. Now that I have grown old enough to fully appreciate the human sexual act in all its passion and splendor, its physical charms and groping intimacies, its mental and absolute spiritual essentialness, now that I have finally arrived at life's all-you-ever-wanted buffet, I can't have any.

MY OLD FRIEND Rusty has embarked upon his first sexual liaison outside his twenty-five-year marriage. He is a changed person. He has taken to wearing flashy ties and fancy shirts and exotic leather shoes. He splashes on an array of colognes and aftershaves that linger about him like a taint. His latest trick is to go out and get his thinning blond hair curled. He insists this mystery lover of his, this whole fantastic carnal episode, has revived his sinking spirits.

Last night the boy was in impeccable form. I joined him for a beer at The Chimes near the north gates of L.S.U. The Chimes is a loud, smoke-filled beer garden and eatery frequented by students and faculty and a few locals who come to admire the scenery. Rusty is a big man who barely fits on the wooden stools designed for narrow-assed college kids. He sat precariously, trying to assess every female in the joint.

"Wouldn't that be something?" he said, eyeing the splendid blonde coed sitting across from us. "I bet her boyfriend doesn't sleep a wink at night. Look at her."

The blonde coed caught us staring and turned away.

Shoo, fly.

"Oooooh," moaned Rusty. "She's good and she knows it."

"Two frogs greet the princess," I said, feeling the pang of her dismissal.

"You're avoiding my question," Rusty said. "I asked if you ever had a flesh-and-blood goddess sit naked in your lap and make you scream?"

"What's the relevance of the question?"

"Then tell me this, Gatlin," he said, "when was the last time you had sex in a moving vehicle in broad daylight?"

"I refuse to answer that."

"Do you remember being sixteen and so sick with lust your stomach hurt? Running your hands up under their tight cotton sweaters? Rolling around in the backseat of a car half the night, French kissing? A four-hour erection. Balls so blue, they hummed a tune."

"That was thirty years ago, Rusty. Where are you going with this?"

"I feel good again," he said. "I never felt so good."

CLIFF IS A NEW FRIEND. A funny, verbose redhead who fled his hometown of Vicksburg four years ago only to become way-laid by bad times here in Baton Rouge. He rents a two-room office suite in the same downtown high rise as I. His wife of two decades left him last summer after walking unannounced into his office and finding him entwined with his secretary. Cliff claimed he was only demonstrating a Roman wrestling clench, but the wife's lawyer made a fool of him at the divorce trial. Just when he thought things had hit rock bottom, his now ex-wife packed up their three kids and moved back to Vicksburg, making regular visitation even more complicated. Cliff believes her intent is to turn the children against him. Punish him for his wanton ways.

Cliff is fond of getting both his strong, freckled hands on your person, relating some convoluted old joke and then squeezing you till you laugh. Once you laugh, he normally lets go. And Cliff, I believe, is in single-minded pursuit of Rusty's new ladylove. He, too, speaks in gushing tones of a colorful Madame X and of the looping heights of her passion.

Cliff was waiting for me in the lobby when I arrived at the office this morning. It was early but he already sported a sly, puckish look. He cornered me against the mailboxes, his face leaning into mine.

"That woman like to broke every large bone in my poor spent body," he said. "She turned me up and back and every way but loose, then rolled me over and sat *down* on my face. Manslaughter is a crime back home in Mississippi. It's not legal to cripple somebody just for acting like a man."

Cliff put one freckled hand high up on my shoulder and began probing the knotted muscles with his thumb.

"There's nothing, Gatlin, nothing this side of China can top that," he said. "It's like drowning in a deep pool with an auburn-haired beauty thrashing in your arms. Like throwing yourself out a high window and wanting to pass out before you hit the earth."

"It won't last," I said, trying to step away from him. "You know that? If you tried to live on a day-to-day basis like that, you would both go crazy."

"This is lust, son, pure, untrammeled lust," he said, jerking me by the arm. "She makes love like she's satisfying some awful grudge, some deep down soulful hurt. Which I figure she is. When she gets it out of her system, she'll call it quits."

"Just like that?" I said.

"Just like that," he said. "She's no ordinary lady."

"And that's all right with you?"

"What I think or feel has nothing to do with it, son."

"So tell me, Cliff, how do you turn your emotions on and off like that?"

"You're confusing sex with sentiment," he said. "This is uncomplicated, shameless sex. You should try it sometime."

* * *

A DISCERNING READER might conclude all this second-hand sex is giving me pause. That I might envy in others the pleasures of keen sensation and great appetite, that something in my life must be lacking. That I am only human.

And being by nature a lover of good puzzles, I cannot help but ponder the identity of the esteemed Madame X, mystery lady of loud limitless orgasms, arbiter of sexual mayhem, lusty lioness.

I should tell you Rusty and Cliff seem perfectly unaware of each other's involvement with the fair lady, and that neither of them, in fact, has ever so much as mentioned her name. It's only my rank speculation, my triangulation of certain clues, selected hints, that leads me to a possible identification.

If my guess is correct, Madame X and her estranged husband are longtime clients of mine. As their financial advisor, I confer with them periodically as to the status of their ongoing investments and college funds — accounts which, for reasons of their own, they continue to hold jointly. Now that the husband has cast aside his family obligations and wandered off in search of his cur-ish self, their home belongs to her. Let's call her Madeline. It happens that Madeline's house is located two streets down from Rusty's domicile. And Cliff, my new friend from Mississippi, resides in the same neighborhood.

So when Rusty and Cliff relate odd details of their sexual exploits with an unnamed neighbor, certain parallels emerge: What are the chances of there being two green-eyed, auburn-haired women in south Baton Rouge who at the height of sexual fervor emit high-pitched yips?

It doesn't take a crime sleuth to figure that Cliff and Rusty have converged upon the same hot-blooded female — a former college beauty with a much-rumored reputation for topless sunbathing on the patio. Madeline fits the lusty profile. I feel it in my bones.

ON MY DRIVE to work earlier this morning, all the women were singing. I do not exaggerate. Every woman I passed or who, as was more often the case, passed me, was singing. And singing, or so it seemed to me, the same joyful song. Their heads bobbed in unison, their fingers tapped their steering wheels in time to the same inscrutable beat. I tried to find their tune on the radio but nothing fit, so I decided they were singing with each other. Imagine. Dozens of freshly bathed, newly coifed, expensively scented women singing their way into work. The blissful song of highway maidens.

Men are more like snarling brutes. On their way to work, men sit sulking behind the wheel, their shoulders hunched, grimacing at the wide world. Many of them pick their noses, thumbs and forefingers stuffed to the first knuckle. Each and every one of them glares hatefully as he passes.

Ride on loathsome rider. Ride on.

Something else I notice: The throng of secretaries working the phones and computer terminals in my office building are all young women. *Young* women — girls practically —you might think we were operating a work-study program for high school coeds. Give them each an armload of textbooks and a stick of gum to chew and you wouldn't know the difference. The young women stay out late with their boyfriends every night of the week only to arrive at work in the morning with puffy eyes and out of breath. For reasons unclear to me, all of them wear thick masks of garish makeup and raccoon eye shadow, bringing to mind a troop of oriental dancers. I expect to walk into the building one morning and find them outfitted in silk kimonos and ceremonial fans. They have taut young skin and firm bosoms and seem completely unaware of the torment they are causing me. Some of them are still wearing braces on their teeth.

I am now officially the oldest person working on the premises. The presiding old coot. The last howling Mohican of south Baton Rouge. All the young secretaries call me *Sir.*

Goddamnit.

MY OFFICE building in downtown Baton Rouge affords one of the finest panoramas in all of the city — a view high above the mighty brown Mississippi, facing west. As my suite occupies the southwest corner of the building, I can also look out across the city toward the L.S.U. campus and University Lake. One of the older, more affluent parts of town, south Baton Rouge sits beneath a lush canopy of semitropical rain forest. Sunlight filters through the trees towering over the old neighborhoods, bathing the world below with copper and gold light. Song birds glide across the green, manicured lawns. Squirrels, possums, raccoons and hoot owls inhabit the backyards and alleyways. Life here is abundant, festive, cast in a fluttering blue tunnel of shadow. Winters are mild.

Once a week or so during the spring of each year, Rusty and I will extend the lunch hour with a slow drive through the L.S.U. campus. There amidst the live oaks and blooming azaleas and red tile Spanish roofs, we are apt to encounter any number of old friends and business associates, themselves out for a spin in gold-green light. The whole scene on campus is like a sprawling outdoor carnival — bands of shouting youth playing pitch and catch, couples strolling hand-in-hand beneath the live oaks, the quarter-hour chiming of the big clock atop the Campanile, the occasional lone coed basking in the sun. As the days grow warmer and the students shed their mild winter clothing for the scant gear of early summer, the frequency of chance encounters between non-students escalates. A stranger to the campus might well wonder at the midday procession of hooting middle-aged men in expensive suits driving round and round the Parade Ground, their heads shot out the windows at all angles.

Campus Security has long since documented this seasonal influx of halting traffic — not to mention the increased incidence of rear-end collisions — but has yet to propose a viable solution.

"Jesus H. Christ. Do you see what I see?"

"No, no, look there. Over there by the flagpole."

"Watch out!"

This morning, I decide to do nothing. Just sit here and stare out my office window. Slip my shoes off, shut and lock the outer door, gaze into the pale-blue western sky. Regard the songbirds sailing round the lush courtyard below me. Survey the river traffic's slow crawl. Hide and watch.

In a bottom drawer of my desk, I find a large envelope

filled with old photographs. A black-and-white shot of me as a child sitting on my father's lap. Assorted pictures of my sister and me as young children. A batch of glossy five-by-sevens of Sarah and me holding hands at our sunny backyard-wedding twenty-something years ago. Color snapshots of the two of us clowning at the beach. Christmas at her parents' house. We look so young and skinny and perfect for each other. Sex and horny youth oozing from every pore. I remember thinking her skin smelled like angel food cake. Her long black hair cast upon a white pillow.

It's Sarah's view that had we raised a child somewhere along the rocky way, our life together would have taken on a grander intent. A child, she claims, would have deflected much of the rancor between us, given us something to work and live for, a resolve. Who can say? I keep telling her we have just gotten older and more set in our mulish ways, with or without issue, but this is only playing into her hand. It's also her contention that I have become a selfish old crank. She insists I've swapped my youthful idealism for a crack at mediocrity and the trivial pursuit of money.

Sarah's latest scheme is for the two of us to drop everything and travel out west, put in an extended holiday at some picturesque spot outside Taos or Santa Fe. Where, I suppose, we would hobnob with other displaced, self-searching, middle-aged couples. Commune with sacred stones and lonesome desert spirits. Go native.

I would rather stay in Baton Rouge and starve to death. Here, at least, I know who can be trusted.

Chapter 2

As of six o'clock this morning, I abandoned all television. And not merely the witless watching of charged particles across the rectangular screen but physical possession as well. I liberated it. I pulled the plug and lugged the set out to the trash cans. Tossed in the remote control gadget and aluminum stand. Had a little farewell, tearless ceremony there at the curb. My boob tube and me. Gave the thing a swift kick in its metallic innards for good measure. It was discovered and hauled away within minutes. An alert junketeer with his new-found marvel.

A pox upon his viewing.

Its absence, to be sure, will foster change. Without the dubious benefit of dozens of channels beaming nonstop into the repose of my living room, I plan to go to bed at a respectable hour. (My cavalcade of gruesome nightmares gets an earlier showing.) Sarah and I will now take our meals in the kitchen without distraction, seated round a properly laid table. Our ongoing squabbles over sex and what to do with the rest of our lives will become less volatile, more expansive, exhibiting a conversational ebb and flow. It will simply be a matter of staying calm, waiting for the appropriate opening, then getting my licks in.

Sarah and I do *talk* to each other. No problems there. We must spend the better part of our lives hashing things out, settling accounts. We converse in the middle of the night if necessary. Neither of us is above waking the other if a salient point is to be made. It's as if by compensating for a possible decline in physical intimacy, our relationship grows increasingly verbal. Is that true? Is there some bizarre corollary here? Language, the spoken word, taking precedence over sweet caress? Let me turn that around: If I were to try putting a lid on it, cease trying to always get in the last conclusive word, stop talking, would I better my chances?

"What's got you so huffy?" Sarah asked, perched above this morning's bowl of crunchy bran nuggets.

Sarah is the only person I've ever met who can roll out of bed and look stunning. Her eyes looked as blue as the sea.

"All I said was 'Happy Birthday, Gatlin'," she said. "You're acting like an old grouch."

"I am not an old grouch," I replied, spooning runny golden egg onto my toast. "What I said was I'm losing my edge, my ability to appreciate things."

"Things?"

"People, places, smells, tastes. Everything's fading."

"You are wearing your new glasses?"

"We're not discussing my eyesight, Sarah."

"You're half blind and vain as a palace peacock," she

said. "It would be just like you to stumble through life rather than wear your new glasses."

"I'm wearing the damned glasses. O.K.? We're not talking about the glasses any more. All right? We're talking about death, deterioration."

My eyesight is a recent casualty — a slow dimming of the soul's outward lights. Suddenly, after half a lifetime of keen, unaided vision, all objects beyond thirty feet have turned to smeared, incoherent images. Faces I've known for decades are unrecognizable across a small room. I cannot read the road signs. It seems the intricate network of muscles, tendons, lenses, ropes, pulleys and bones responsible for focusing at a distance has grown lazy, unwilling to put in an honest day's work. The result, not surprisingly, is a new pair of prescription glasses sitting on the bridge of my nose. Something else for my already crowded shirt pocket. One more item, along with keys, wallet, money clip, business cards, pens, pocket calendar and briefcase, to keep up with. One more glaring symbol of my downward slide.

"Well, I hope you're not heading for some kind of crack-up," Sarah said, helping herself to another spoonful of rocks.

"Crack-up? What's that supposed to mean?"

"Crack-up, crisis, call it what you want. Women accept their mortality better than men."

I had a good idea where Sarah was going with this but I didn't know how I could stop her.

"Some sort of biological advantage?" I said.

"Maybe," she said. "But I really think men define themselves in terms of their physical prowess. A weakening of strength threatens your identity."

"And women are above *that?* So what's all this commotion with face lifts and tummy tucks and skin creams you ladies are so fond of? Name one woman we know who doesn't color her hair."

"The preservation of one's natural looks and the fear of dying are separate and distinct," Sarah said, brushing her black bangs off her high forehead. "Men see decline and fear death. Women are more accepting."

"Let's assume, Sarah, let's assume for the moment that women are more accepting. A harsh wind blows and the tall, supple grasses of womanhood bend accordingly. So how does that make you any better than us? Tell me."

"I didn't say women were better, just different," she said. "Besides, without me, you would have fallen off the edge of the earth long ago."

Sarah stopped chewing and stared at me.

"And Gatlin," she said, "please use your napkin. You've got egg on your chin."

THERE ARE pivotal moments along the continuum of our lives here on Planet Earth. We act and are therefore not the same people we were moments before. Last Saturday, in the yellow spangled light of dawn, four days before my forty-seventh birthday, while standing in the cash only checkout line at the local Bet-R store, I became a crusty old bastard. It was easy.

Mind you, I did not come looking for trouble. I came in for fresh trout fillets, a green bell pepper, six red potatoes and a bunch of shallots. What I discovered was loutish youth all done up in a bow tie and a blue apron behind a cash register. But I'm telling it too fast.

On weekends, holidays and special occasions, when Sarah and I are not partaking of some low-salt, no-fat swill out of cardboard boxes or aluminum cans, we like to indulge ourselves. Seafood is our first choice: Shrimp Creole, Shrimp Scampi, Shrimp Au Gratin, Redfish Courtbouillon, Oysters Bienville, Oysters Rockefeller, Oysters en brochette, barbecued shrimp, boiled shrimp, boiled crabs, broiled red snapper, seafood gumbo, grilled redfish, crawfish pie, crawfish étouffée, stuffed flounder, stuffed crab, seafood stuffed eggplant, panfried speckled trout.

It puts me in a good mood just pronouncing the names of these dishes. I wake early on the rare feast day and plan my menu, what seasonings I'll need, what vegetables will work, what kind of bread to buy, what wine will go with what. It is to be a day of cooking, a day of collaboration, intuition, experimentation and wine tasting (a cup of wine for the gumbo, a cup for the cook!) culminating in a candle-lit gourmet dinner for two with my long-legged spouse. If I'm very lucky, passions will be stirred.

I write everything I'll need for dinner on a list, double check it, then head out early to beat the crowds. I arrive at the grocery store in a state of near exaltation, eager, confident, emboldened. This is not shopping, this is art.

It was in such a humor that I arrived at the checkout line last Saturday morning with my few purchases of fish fillets, potatoes, bell pepper and shallots. To save time, I pulled into the *Cash Only* line — *Eight Items or Less*. Behind the register, an outbreak of plum-colored acne spattered across his downy cheeks, stood my nemesis.

"I'm sorry, sir," he said. "You'll have to go through a full-service line."

"Pardon?"

"I can't check you out, sir. You'll have to go to another line."

And with that the bepimpled youth turned his back on me and gazed out across the nearly vacant supermarket. At this hour of the morning there was no one shopping but me and a couple of old codgers who had nothing better to do.

"What's the problem?" I said.

"This is the 'cash only' line, sir."

"I've got ten thousand dollars in cash in my pocket, son, just ring me up."

"You're over the limit," he said.

His tone of voice was accusatory, as if I were trying to smuggle a ham out under my shirt.

"What are you talking about?" I said.

"This is the 'cash only' line — eight items or less," the youth said. "You have nine."

"Nine?"

"Yes, sir. If you'll just step over to one of the full-service lines, they'll be glad to help you."

"Now hold on a second," I said. "This is a package of fish fillets, these are some potatoes, this is a bell pepper, this is a bunch of shallots. That's four. Count them."

Rarely were the scales of righteousness so heavily tilted in one's favor. The youth stared at my groceries, then smiled warily.

"The fish is one, sir, the pepper is two, the shallots are three, together with six potatoes that makes nine. The limit is eight."

Caught off-guard, I was unprepared for the jolt of thundering rage that shook my limbs. I wanted to slap the young punk across the pimples.

"It's six o'clock in the morning," I said, forcing myself to articulate each word carefully. "The store's practically empty, and you expect me to stand here and haggle over the number of fucking potatoes I'm buying?"

"The limit is eight items, sir," he said smugly.

"And I have nine?"

"Yes, sir. You have nine."

I reached out, took hold of one of the red potatoes (it fit in my hand as perfectly as a new baseball), stepped back and hurled the spud as far as I could into the dark depths of the supermarket. It landed with a dull *puufffmmuh* sound — not unlike the concussion of a distant mortar round — followed by the faint tinkling of broken glass.

"There," I said. "Eight items. Now ring it up!"

YESTERDAY, ANOTHER milestone on the road to infirmity. I was strolling back to my office after a hasty lunch at Po' Boy Lloyd's (tepid, limp lettuce leaves soaked in diet salad dressing) when I stepped off the curb onto a pea-sized stone, twisted my ankle and sprawled face down in the middle of the intersection. It was my first ground-level view of the central business district. Oncoming pedestrians averted their eyes and changed course, irate motorists gunned their engines and awaited the removal of the hindrance in the street. Out of nowhere appeared two nimble retirees to assist the possibly drunk, dismayed pilgrim to his feet and over to the bus-stop bench. Though hobbled, it was my pride that suffered most.

Did a walk down the city street become problematic at forty-seven? Should I avoid curbs? Perhaps a cane for getting up and down flights of stairs?

"Poor Mr. Pitiful," Sarah said, closing the top of the cereal box.

I've noticed the more gritty, dirt-like the cereal, the more Sarah likes it.

"I wish you would stop saying that, Sarah."

"Then stop acting so pitiful. Today's your birthday and I need a clue, some little hint as to what to get you."

"It's no fun picking out your own present."

"I never said I was going to give you what you asked for," she said. "I'm looking for categories. What about something for the kitchen?"

A little *something* for the kitchen is exactly what I did not need. We must own every vegetable-slicing, fruit-juicing, food-dicing kitchen contraption ever created by mankind.

"I was thinking along the lines of the bedroom, Sarah. Something long and tall with a moist, dark center."

"Poor Mr. Pitiful."

This ongoing battle of wits has a certain rhythm to it. Thrust and parry, retreat, attack, touché.

"What's so pitiful about wanting to make love to your wife?" I said. "Has that gone out of fashion, too? Is in-home celibacy next on the political agenda?"

"This is boring," she said. "Next topic."

"Sex is boring?"

"You beat it to death, dear. Let's talk about our summer vacation plans."

"It's *my* birthday, Sarah. I don't want to talk about packing off into the high desert for spiritual rekindling."

"Speak for yourself," she said. "I'm suffocating."

"What's that supposed to mean?"

"Suffocating? It's a word, dear. It means to be stifled or smothered."

"I know what it means," I said. "How does it apply to you?"

Sarah looked straight across the table into my eyes.

"I am not happy," she said. "I do not share in your contented bliss. I want a change. I think we *both* need a change."

SARAH, my wife, lover and verbal combatant these past twenty-four years, is like the rare tropical butterfly that lives for an hour and then dies. For her, life should be lived as a spontaneous, all-consuming rush, with nothing before or after. She's as whimsical as a sprite. If she wakes one sky-blue morning and decides to spend the day reading in bed, she cancels all her plans and does it. No gas in the car? She rides her bike to the store. No ongoing spectacle in her life? Time to chuck everything and wander out to Santa Fe.

She is, without question, the most confounding person I have ever known. A tall, long-legged, always casually, if meticulously dressed (and I have the credit-card receipts to prove it), striking woman with flawless, fair skin and dark blue eyes, Sarah has grown more attractive with age. A skinny, boisterous, ordinary girl becomes glamorous over time. She is one of the more quick-witted, well-scrubbed persons you will ever meet. She must shower four times a day. She likes people and cannot make a quick trip to the hardware store without bumping into half-a-dozen friends and acquaintances amidst the bric-a-brac. She is nobody's fool.

It is to Sarah's mind that I direct my criticism — or rather to her knack for changing her mind whenever it suits her. Beneath that winsome, well-scrubbed face of hers rests a brain that can turn on a dime. Rather than bounding about the mirrored studio with her barking, white-robed karate instructor, she will elect to commune with her innermost self via t'ai chi. Having settled ourselves to a birthday breakfast, she declares her intention of traveling (without me if necessary) out west to where the cowboys ride and sing. Gone to the hardware store to buy birdseed, she will return home with half-a-dozen azalea bushes.

Once planted, however, the azaleas are of no more concern to Sarah than last summer's caladium bulbs rotting in the back bed. *Live or die*, that's Sarah's credo of gardening. She cannot be bothered with such things as pruning, watering and weeding. That's my job.

Don't misread me, Sarah is a kind, thoughtful person possessed of a strong will and a potent love for her friends and family. If ever a heavy stone were required to be lifted to a high hill, Sarah could be counted on to get it there. She has a keen, if sometimes stinging, sense of humor. Without her, my life would be sorely unhinged.

What Sarah and I always had in common was good sex. Good, strong, acrobatic sex. We made love on trains, on planes, on the floors of our friends' guest rooms, in the backyard under the moon and stars. We attacked each other with fruits and vegetables and assorted fragrant gels and scented oils. We drove each other to unspeakable heights of desire and rump-smacking satisfaction. We did it wherever, whenever, possible. But the furnace that drove the engine cooled.

One morning in her mid-thirties, Sarah awoke and announced we ought to have a child. A big-eyed baby, it suddenly occurred to her, would give direction to our dispirited, complicated lives, would fill full our carelessly luffing sails. She decided it was time we made amends for our fornicating ways. Out of habit, I felt obliged to disagree with her. Taking the low road, I argued that children were sickly, noisy, demanding and expensive, and offered no guarantee of marital concord, and that unlike many of our close friends with small children, we got to sleep late on weekends.

Sarah would have none of it. She began to greet the onset of each succeeding month's menstrual flow with increasing torment and despair, as if her own body were conspiring against her, against us. Before I knew it, our once rollicking life together was being held hostage to an idea, a fanciful home movie playing solely at the back of Sarah's obstinate mind.

And then one sunny day in spring at age thirty-eight, Sarah discovered herself pregnant, and for the next ten weeks or so went marching off to a never-never land of baby clothes and crib toys and child development books. A shining star had fallen into her waiting womb and taken root. But her rapture was not to last. In the middle of her third month, Sarah suffered a miscarriage and was brought plummeting back to earth. A number of failed pregnancies over the next half-dozen years put an end to the notion of parenthood as the means of redeeming a frenetic lifestyle.

After her final pregnancy, once we unpacked our hospital bags, sealed our minds, one of the chores confronting us was the dismantling of the nursery. In a fit of enthusiasm, Sarah had scrubbed and painted the spare bedroom, installed a baby bed and matching furniture, affixed cardboard renditions of Mother Goose characters to walls and ceiling. Cartoon figures adorned the iridescent drapes. From the overhead light fixture wheeled a mobile of brightly painted farm animals. A profusion of primary colors that made me wince.

In an hour or so the baby furniture was disassembled and safely stored in the garage and the nursery was returned to its former state of guest room, none the worse for wear in light of the new coat of pale-blue paint. It is a pleasant room with a firm bed for a traveler to lay his head.

But the question of issuance, or rather of our failure to bring it off, was never put to rest. We became coconspirators in an unspoken pledge not to discuss it. Privately at least, Sarah became less flamboyant, not so girlish, and slightly aloof. And slowly more beautiful. As a married couple we tightened our communal belts, executed a succession of spiraling mortgages and muddled on. Separately, we each drew well-entrenched battle lines and settled in for the long haul.

The jolly good fight.

"IT'S NO WONDER you're depressed," Sarah said, rinsing her cereal bowl at the sink.

"I'm not depressed."

"Who wouldn't be?" she said. "Living in this hellhole."

"I like living in Baton Rouge."

"It's a polluted landfill lorded over by a legislature full of ignorant goons."

"It's no different anywhere else, Sarah."

"It's a zoo," she said. "The economy has collapsed. It's too humid. L.S.U. has been overrun by a bunch of arrogant, overpaid Yankees. Every other person you meet is a lawyer."

"Some of our best friends are lawyers."

"If we had the courage," she said, "we would pack the car and go."

"Courage? This is my livelihood you're talking about. My business."

"Let's sell it," she said. "We'll take the money from the business and the income from my trust and make a clean break. It's more than enough money. It's too much. Let's get out of here while we can."

"We have a life here," I said, tossing my cloth napkin toward the sink. "I've got clients who seek my financial advice and many of them actually *take it*. Does that surprise you? They give me their money and I look after it. It's what I do. And your family's *here*. Our friends are here. What about them?"

"Friends?" she said. "You mean that league of strangers that meets three or four times a year whether it wants to or not? I hardly know what to say to them anymore. And neither do you. If we didn't have their children to talk about, we wouldn't talk at all."

Sarah, to be fair, is dead on regarding our circle of old college friends. What began as a network of small fissures across the lush landscape of our affections has broadened into an arid no man's land. We get together infrequently for drinks and the obligatory barbecues, exchange pleasantries, gossip — amid much, much smiling. After one of these gatherings my cheek muscles ache from smiling. What's missing is a sense of ingenuousness. I honestly fear we will all gather around the smoking briquettes one gold-green afternoon and have nothing left to say to each other.

I knew things were really amiss when my old friends begin introducing their new friends. I sat there like some distant dimwit relative come to Christmas dinner who didn't know a goddamn soul. I got a seat at the grownup table all right, but the conversation took place in the present. And I was part of the past.

The irony is I enjoy the children of my old friends more than ever. I can talk to them. Given the chance, they will tell me about the books they are reading, what they hope to make of their lives.

SARAH PUT her cereal bowl in the dishwasher and walked to the refrigerator, removing a carton of orange juice.

"Look," she said, "just because we go away for a time doesn't mean we won't come back. Where's your sense of fun?"

"Pardon me, Sarah, but I have trouble equating a sense of fun with the idea of roaming the great Wild West like an exile. I like the life I've got here."

"And there you are," she said, sitting back down across from me. "You like the life you've got here. Your business. Your friends. This trip is for me."

"At last we're getting down to a real sense of things."

"Maybe you're right," she said, tapping a fingernail against the side of her juice glass. "Maybe you should stay in Baton Rouge and run your business, keep up with your old friends, and I'll go out west. It was my idea to begin with. You stay here and I'll go."

"If I didn't know better, I might think you were serious about this."

"You can take it to the bank," she said, finishing off her orange juice.

"Allow me to point out, Sarah, that we're a married couple, and that married couples don't just split up whenever it suits them. Married people go places, take trips together. I mean, you go gallivanting off into the wild frontier and anything could happen."

"That's more or less the point, Gatlin."

I stood up, walked over to where my napkin lay on the floor by the sink. I picked it up, folded it and put it on the counter.

"Where is it you want to go," I asked. "To do what?"

"You're still missing the point," she said. "The purpose is just to go. To wander, to explore. Why do you have such a problem with that? What are you afraid of?"

"I'm not afraid."

"Then what's stopping you?" she said, standing and pitching her empty juice glass into the sink.

The crash of shattering glass was like a punch in the face.

"What's got you backed up in a corner all moody and distracted?" she asked. "You're getting black circles under your eyes."

* * *

BLACK CIRCLES under the eyes are a familial trait, like big ears, flat feet, long noses. A casual examination of photographs of my family reveals a progression of glaring, black-eyed men and women peering back into the camera lens. The black circles lend a slight vulnerability to their overall peevish stares.

My father was no exception, either in looks or temperament. Sometimes I think he simply wore himself out — all those rocketing highs and plunging lows having taken their toll on a man with such grand obsessions. As a child, I remember one period during which he became fixated on the threat of nuclear attack. The idea of war consumed him like a virus. He devoured stacks of books and articles about the bomb; he hoarded water and food supplies in the toolshed above the garage. He walked the floors and waited for the air raid sirens. He had difficulty sleeping.

He once spent an entire Sunday afternoon huddled over a parish road map on which he diagrammed the blast zones radiating out from the center of downtown like ripples on a small pond. He told us he was plotting our chances.

"This first circle," explains my father, "marks the outer edge of the crater."

"What's a crater?" asks my younger sister.

"It's a big hole in the ground. Everything standing inside this first circle will be vaporized by the bomb."

"What's vaporized?"

"Everything inside here will be blown to dust," he says. "A fine, white radioactive dust. Poof."

"Where's our house?"

My father leans back over his bomb map, repositions his protractor and inscribes a small red *X*.

"Right about here," he says.

"Let me see!" says my sister, pushing me out of her way.

The red *X* lies well within the confines of the first circle. My father sets aside his mapping tools and purses his lips. After what seems like minutes, he lets go his breath.

"We'll be blown upon the wind, children. There will be nothing left."

My sister starts to wail.

During the coming months, while much of America begins a frenzy of fallout-shelter construction and disaster planning, our father sits around watching television, waiting for the blinding-white flash. He tells my sister and me the joyride is over.

"Show's over, kids. It's all over but the crying."

Our mother says at least we know what's going to happen to us.

"If the missiles come," she says, "if the mad Russians let the hammer fly, death will be certain and instantaneous. But it will be painless. We won't feel a thing."

The notion of a swift and fiery end seemed to bolster our father's darkest fears. He put away his bomb map and never mentioned the holocaust again. He sank into a slow, twisting slide. He bought a handgun from the back pages of a hunting magazine and stashed it in his bedroom. He began to drink openly and to excess. He took to staying up nights watching the stars and sleeping days.

Chapter 3

In this morning's office mail comes a remembrance. Greetings from my auto mechanic. Sid, on behalf of the entire staff at Auto-Care, wishes me the happiest of birthdays and invites me in for a tune-up. (Does he mean me or my car?) It would be easy to dismiss Sid's gesture excepting the fact that few in my association have so much as picked up the telephone. We cling to those who remember us.

Enter here the remaining member of my circle of middle-aged comrades: Rick Creel. Unlike some I can name, he is not sleeping with Madame *X*, siren of the suburbs. Rick has tempered his once-raging melancholia to a cat's purr. Events of recent years have turned in his favor, conferring upon him a mantle of purpose and rigorous self-control. He shuns alcohol, tobacco, drugs, the use of harsh language, carbonated drinks, red meat, tropical oils, all processed foods, butter, eggs, sugar and salt. He has ceased squandering his time on muddled pursuits. With his close-cropped hair, black beard and deep-set brooding eyes, his physical presence has taken on a stern, almost ascetic look. A kind of upbeat Abe Lincoln in wrinkled khakis.

Rick recently parted ways with the hierarchy of city government and its patchwork social agenda and has now thrown in with a nonprofit group that occupies a refurbished storefront down by the river. Here amid the lingering squalor of downtown Baton Rouge, Rick and his fellow activists have fashioned a combination homeless mission, arts center, halfway house and secular place of worship. Rick's shaggy band of malcontents and social activists have somehow pulled it off, put their vast differences aside and built a place to come together. Among the center's largely volunteer staff is a contingent of left-leaning students and faculty from L.S.U., all of whom share a fervent, egalitarian view of the world and, on the whole, keep their personal opinions to themselves. Rick is one of their leaders. He leadeth them by running water. And he has great concern for me. About my person he detects a mustering rot.

"You look like you've been beaten with a large stick this morning," Rick observes from the opposite side of my desktop. "Birthday boy had another bad night?"

"Sleep has become a fitful dozing," I say, "replete with bad dreams and wailing voices."

Rick studies me with his fierce black eyes as if he can read my nightmares and marital woes.

"If you're hounded by dreams," he says, "you ought to try remembering them. Keep a journal. Jot them down at night and then look at them later. See if you can detect a pattern. Do something."

That's my friend Rick for you. Give him an opening and he'll move in and set up housekeeping.

"What I do, Rick, is lie there dreaming like a banshee. When I can't sleep, I listen to my heart pound."

"Sounds like a meltdown."

"A Chernobyl of the mind," I say, wishing it wasn't so.

RICK'S SENSE of agitated well-being is almost palpable. He sits brooding there in one of my leather office chairs, stroking his scruffy black beard, watching me squirm. Abe Lincoln reviews his troops.

"I'm not recommending you to *save* anyone or anything," he says. "All I'm suggesting is volunteering a few hours of your time each week. Find some way to lend a hand and then do it. Look at it this way, Gatlin, it might get your mind off your own problems."

"What makes you think I've got problems?"

"You're the one who's plagued by nightmares. You fret like a caged animal."

Rick is forever telling me my biggest problem is that I am not engaged in the present moment. That I am being confounded by the demands of my job and the fireworks of my own emotions, that I am a man blinded by his own riches.

"As always, Rick, I appreciate the unflinching critique of my character. All this coming from a man who once mooned the Dean of Women at Homecoming."

Rick rejects my sally with a wave of his hand.

"That was a long time ago and I had been drinking," he says.

"You were bombed out of your mind. Both of us were. But the point is, you're not seeing my side of things. You're not out in the real world every day fighting a hungry bear with a switch."

"You exaggerate," Rick says, laughing. "You twist everything so far out of proportion, it's no longer recognizable. You always have. Just slow down and enjoy life. It's your birthday, isn't it? Relax. What's the point of all the hard work if it causes you such aggravation?"

"You make it sound as if this business of mine runs itself."

"Doesn't it?"

"One bad quarter and the whole thing is history. I'm like a man walking around with a live grenade strapped to his chest."

"Enough already," he says. "Look, I just dropped by for the fellowship. The advice was free."

RICK'S LATEST crusade is to get me to go to Angola with him. No longer satisfied consorting with disaffected students and intellectuals, the homeless, the drunk and drugged, wastrels of every stripe and hue, Rick wants *me* to accompany him up to the State Penitentiary and put on a little show for the inmates.

What Rick has in mind is a live presentation — a short skit for two characters — to be staged for the benefit of selected felons and prison staff. Rick will assume the lead, I am to appear as the sole supporting cast member — a largely symbolic role, he assures me — with few lines and a limited emotional range. The idea is for the two of us to travel up to Angola tomorrow morning, meet with the newly created drama club, then put on the skit. Hopefully, it will generate some interesting discussion.

"God? You want me to play God? It's damn kind of you to ask, Rick, but God? Jesus."

"No," he says. "You'll be God, and I'll play his son. No dreary St. Peter, no archangels, no teeming multitudes. And definitely no wise men. Just you and me. God and his erratic number one son."

"You're the one with the beard, Rick," I say, shuffling through a stack of printouts. "You play God. Just count me out. I've got a lot of work to do *here*. I can't be running up and down the countryside entertaining every killer and armed robber in sight. It's just too weird."

"I'll get you a beard," he says. "I'll get you whatever you need. And don't try to tell me you couldn't stand to get away from the stock market for a day. Look, do me this one favor. I need your help. We can leave midmorning and be back before dark. I'll drive."

THE TORMENTS of others often escape us and yet no one avoids his turn in the barrel, including Rick. After years of smoldering conflict, Rick's seventeen-year-old stepson has stormed out of the house vowing to return only upon the death, removal or capitulation of his stepfather. Since neither of these events is forthcoming, Matt is living in a friend's garage apartment for the summer. Matt lied about his age and got a job on one of the crew boats servicing the big ships on the Mississippi. He now fancies himself a real seaman and plans to one day join the merchant marines and sail across the sea. As I have known him since he was a boy and impose few restraints on his language or lofty ambitions, Matt has taken to dropping by my office on his lunch hour to talk about his new life on the river. Today is no exception.

Matt sits across from me in the same leather armchair his stepfather occupied not one hour ago. We make small talk and survey the river traffic out my window. He eats his bag lunch. I drink coffee.

Rising out of Lake Itasca in northern Minnesota, the Mississippi River and its tributaries sweep the soil of thirty-one states, traveling some four thousand miles, before emptying into the Gulf of Mexico. At its mouth, the river pushes half a million cubic feet of chocolate-brown water per second. It is a moving wall of liquid mud.

The Ojibwa tribes of Wisconsin called it *Missi Sipi* or 'Great River.' Columbus may have sighted it on one of his voyages. De Soto is credited with its discovery. La Salle explored it. The kings of Spain and France and later England laid claim to it. The upstart Americans paid cash.

Today the river in Baton Rouge is largely forgotten, a vulgar hangout for dockside gambling boats, scenic backdrop for holiday firework displays, industrial dumping ground. Out of sight and out of the public mind behind its tall earthen restraints. A vast, fast-flowing curiosity.

Having embraced the latest fashion of disgruntled youth, Matt is dressed in unpolished army boots, baggy cut-off pants and a huge faded flannel shirt that drapes about his knees. He's growing a beginner's goatee and his long brown hair is parted in the middle, falling across his shoulders. He wears sunglasses day and night. Unable to sit still, both his feet are drubbing the pile carpet and his hands run up and down the arms of the leather armchair.

"This is utterly fucking it," he says, jumping to his feet and pointing to the Mississippi below us. "This is what I can't stop thinking about. I lie in bed at night and I picture it, I shut my eyes and I see it. I see that big fat sun in the sky, the brown water rushing past. And I can't get it out of my head. You know what I'm saying?"

Sitting high above the river in my downtown office, I am waiting, half-hoping.

"Take a seat, Matt. Keep talking."

"Is this incredible or what?" he says. "Can you spend too much time thinking about blue sky and running water? Am I blowing this whole thing out of proportion?"

"What are you trying to tell me?"

"I'm telling you working out on this river is like getting scot-goddamn-free!" he says, raising both hands in the air. "That's the only word for it. It's all water and sky and sunlight bound up in one. Like being in the center of everything and all of it's moving around *me*, it's all there for the taking. All I've got to do is keep my eyes open, keep my head right, wait. Be still. I'm free and everything else is falling in place. Every last bit of it. You know what I'm saying?"

What would it be like?

"I'm listening, Matt."

"Yesterday I rode one of the crew boats all the way down to the locks at White Castle," Matt says, striding before the window. "The crew captain let me take the wheel for a while.

There I was, man, steering the boat right down the Big Muddy. Free as a bird! We passed the Mississippi Queen steaming her way upriver toward Baton Rouge. All the tourists on the upper deck waving and shooting our pictures. Big red paddle wheel flashing in the sunlight, calliope blaring, river rushing past. It was too much, man. You should have been there."

LIFE IN BATON ROUGE has its limitations. Because of the rich foliage, the surrounding wall of living green, my vision grows weak. I live and die beneath the overhanging rain forest. My senses become choked by the deluge of flower and bloom and bud. Sweet scents permeate my clothing, my hair, the cupboards of my kitchen, the pages of my books. Look up and I see trees. Look around and I see boundaries — giant shrubs or towering hedgerows or thick cane breaks or flourishing green fence lines. There is no escaping it.

The view from my office window, looking west out over the flat, boiling surface of the Mississippi, is something else. I can see. Open my eyes, *look*. I can see as far as I wish, as far as I ever dreamed. Look. I am not accustomed to this. I squint, I strain to focus. My jungle vision has not prepared me for the blue ache of space before me, the flat horizon stretching all the way to Texas. I see with the eyes of fish. I sit with an old friend's errant stepson and witness the river's passing.

RUSTY PHONES me at two o'clock with an update of his love life. I can almost sense his fuming lust and pungent cologne through the receiver.

"After she takes her skirt and panties off, she sits spraddle-legged facing the mirror with a bowl of banana pudding and begins spooning the —"

"So tell me, Rusty, how can you possibly keep them separate?"

"Who?"

"Julie and this ladyfriend of yours. What stops this lusty affair from spilling over into your marriage?"

"Julie and I are getting along just fine," he says. "Both girls made the honor roll again this year. Business is great. Julie is thinking of opening a coffee shop south of campus. The whole family is going to Florida for a week at the end of the month."

"Then why the mistress, Rusty? You're spending one, two afternoons a week with another woman. How's that fit in?"

"It's passion."

All is dead silence on the other end of the phone line, and I wonder if Rusty is thinking of hanging up.

"I said it's passion," he says finally. "It's something I had forgotten. Julie and I have been married since we got out of college. She's had to work full-time, besides looking after the girls. I spent ten years on the road, remember? Ten years living in motel rooms. I wasn't the most help around the home front."

"Until now? Now that you've begun screwing another woman?"

"Let me finish," he says. "A man can't expect his wife to satisfy his every goddamn whim. It's not natural. It's not even realistic. Over time it's normal for certain desires, certain appetites within a marriage to simmer down. No matter how hot the fire, eventually it's got to burn itself out."

And cold are its ashes.

"You're now proposing a theory of marital entropy, is that it, Rusty?"

"Julie and I work our tails off," he says. "It's hard enough just keeping a roof over our heads. There's not enough space, enough time left over for intrigue, for passion. It's too much to ask. Human history tells us that."

"Are you telling me you're having this affair for the sake of your marriage?"

"I'm saying that no relationship is perfect. That men and women live together and do the very best they can."

"I know you, Rusty. I've known you since you were eighteen years old. I introduced you to Julie. You're getting caught up in this wild fling of yours and it's taking over your life. It's all you think about."

"Right this minute," Rusty says, "I've got my mind fixed on a big, heaping bowl of banana pudding!"

THE TROUBLE with a light lunch is by mid-afternoon I feel woozy and obsessed with eating. Easing down to the lobby to purchase a bag of roasted peanuts, I bump into Vicksburg's horniest favorite son. He leans into me, breathing his husky breath.

"Cow's in the sweet corn," Cliff says, grabbing me.

"What?"

"Fire in the henhouse."

"What does that mean, Cliff?"

"Her husband knows she's messing around."

"How can you tell?"

"I caught him watching her house."

"Madame *X*'s? You were there?"

"Buck naked and big as life," he says.

"So what happened?"

"Nothing yet. He may be figuring his next move."

"So what were you doing all this time?"

"Hunting for my socks," he says.

"All undressed and nowhere to hide, huh? Does he know it's you?"

"Beats me. I left out the side door and jumped the fence."

"You think he's watching the house, Cliff? Keeping an eye out for who's slipping by? Doesn't that strike you as peculiar? What would a man in his position hope to gain?"

"I figure it finally dawned on him that somebody is fucking his wife," he says.

SHOULD A MAN FEEL timid having to admit fidelity to his wife of twenty-four years? Is he to be judged as somehow less of a man? Less qualified to address his peers?

Over time I have watched virtually every married man I know wander off his course, floundering in the bog of illicit sex. And the results have been uniformly disastrous. Mind you, it's all stars and fireworks at the outset, cheap thrills and bright lights, all that's meet and right. But then it changes. Despite his vehement claims that sex is only physical, that sex is merely a rowdy poke in the wet and wonderful dark, he becomes attached. The next casualty will be his great good sense.

Yet, I, too, have sexual fantasies — still unrealized, still unpronounced. My heart is a fetid backwater of unrequited lust.

Sidestepping the moral issue for the moment, what are my options?

The obvious, least-perilous course of action is for me to keep my head down and my mouth shut, pretend I know nothing about Cliff and Rusty and the Lady Madeline, and enjoy the ongoing spectacle. Hide and watch, as my father used to say. Sooner or later this three-sided sex engine is going to gather momentum and jump the tracks. Then things will get exciting.

Or, in the spirit of the unabashed voyeur, I can creep a little closer to the action. After all, no one is aware that I have put all the puzzle pieces together. Cliff and Rusty don't even know about each other. If my hunch is correct, I can approach Madeline on a purely professional basis and avoid tipping my hand. In a world without wonder, vicarious pleasure is superior to none.

Or I can throw my own hat into the bedlam of the ring. If the Fairy Queen should wish to lay me under her gossamer wings, who am I to buck?

Part II

Thursday, June 7

Early Morning

Chapter 4

After several hours of ruthless dreaming, I declare fancy the winner and get up and dress. Nothing like starting your day in the dark. Yesterday was my birthday; today, I'm just another willful schmuck.

Arriving downtown in the first light, I take up position at my office window. Slow rolling thunderheads, like huge black dirigibles, roar and rattle the window glass, lightning splits the sky. Dense sheets of rain obscure the river. In the courtyard below me, magnolia leaves leap back and forth in the stiff wet wind as if they are on strings. The grey, brittle limbs of the pecan tree clatter to the ground.

Mr. Pitiful sits high and dry behind his oversized desk and wonders about the birds. How do they manage to survive? Possessed of no material wealth, clothing, culture or religious collateral and yet they flourish. A beak and two wings and a pair of stick feet against the storm's full fury. Where do they go at times like this? What's their queer secret?

Not a bird in sight.

After the storm rolls away, the air is piled in cool, smoky layers around the trees and window ledges. The rain runs in puddles. The roof drips silver jewels.

As the first rays of sunshine peep through the overcast, a visitor happens on the scene. It's the attorney Biggs, Third Street's resident bogeyman. Prior to his mental collapse last winter, Biggs maintained a law office in this very building. He now stalks the downtown area in what outwardly appears to be a hopeless search for his marbles.

Biggs is a spare, disheveled character in a rumpled business suit, cast-off jogging shoes, with a brown paper bag under one arm. His grey-black hair has been hacked off close to his scalp and his fixed, tormented stare bids you look away. He circles from window to window around the courtyard, leering in like a skull on the end of a stick. He shouts out something unintelligible and pummels the side door; he turns and points a finger at the low-flying clouds. Satisfied he has the place to himself, he begins setting out handful after handful of what appears to be birdseed on the packed bare dirt under the trees. He scurries from place to place around the courtyard as fast as his crooked legs can carry him — an unkempt, demented goblin. And then, as abruptly as he appeared, he dashes out of the courtyard and across the puddled street and into the church playground opposite my building. I lose sight of him as he scoots behind a live oak tree.

What brings him my way on this dreary morn?

One day in December of last year, Biggs was discovered kneeling in a corner of the courtyard of our building, talking to himself. Prior to his collapse, Biggs had rented the office space next to mine, stopping by occasionally to shoot the breeze, drink coffee. He was a soft-spoken man in his early fifties who kept to himself, liked L.S.U. sports, had a son living somewhere in the East. His wife of three decades had run off with one of his best friends two years before.

But Biggs was not his usual self that cold December morning. His clothes were filthy, his eyes were round and staring. He became visibly agitated when approached by any of the young secretaries; he tossed a stick at the security guard. Eventually a platoon of sheriff's deputies was summoned and Biggs was carted away for ten days of observation at the city's expense. Upon his release, he took to roving the downtown streets.

As no one knew either the whereabouts of his ex-wife or next of kin, I was nominated to escort the sheriff's deputies to Biggs's crosstown residence after his detainment. Arriving at the house, the deputies and I were greeted with signs of an aborted life. Dozens of yellowed newspapers littered the lawn and sidewalk. Unopened mail spilled out of the box and down across the porch. The front screen door was thrown open, hanging by one hinge. In the backyard, a pack of half-starved looking dogs hurled themselves against the chain-link fence.

Inside the house we discovered someone had taken a hammer or blunt object and smashed all the plates and glasses. Every mirror and picture frame had been given a whacking good crack; the spout of an antique teapot was snapped off cleanly like a thumb. Countless plastic bags of foul-smelling garbage were piled high in the dining room. I declined to inspect the fridge.

Beneath the raised floor of Biggs's house, I heard his dogs scuttling back and forth, fighting for position, jostling the water pipes. I could not resist the image of the bewildered divorcé living out his eerie shadow life while below him his half-wild hounds bickered and prowled, fornicated and drooled: *Up in the night Biggs hears one of the bigger males scratching, clawing at the underside of the house, and he figures it's his trusted old friend trying to dig his way in to get at him. No longer satisfied with the sacking of his wife, his old friend has come back to finish what's left of him. I see the two of them, broken man and raging beast, crouched and circling in the wrecked living room, scarcely breathing, eyes narrowed, hackles raised, waiting for the opening, ready to pounce. One of them must die. The other is mad.*

Last night I dream that Sarah vanishes: I come home early from work and she's packed the car and gone. Vamoosed. Her remains are everywhere. Hair brushes, bobby pins, jars of skin cream. Tweezers, a makeup mirror, earrings. In the bathroom cabinet I find an eyelash curler. What a device! Unsure at first, I try curling my own lashes. Magically two black butterflies land on my face. I blink my eyes and they take flight. I pile on gobs of makeup, draw on beauty spots and a monster scar. Smear on clown cheeks and make funny red lips. Blacken my front teeth.

I wander into the kitchen where I discover a wolfhound standing on his hind legs eating out of the open fridge. He's devouring my leftovers, scattering paper, food scraps and bits of bone onto the floor. His powerful jaws lock and then tear, everything gets gulped whole. He turns to see me standing in the doorway. He licks his chops.

STREWN ACROSS the kitchen table when I arrived home last night was an assortment of colorful maps depicting the western

United States. Beside the maps lay a new leather shaving kit with a big red bow and birthday balloons attached. No subtlety here. Sarah stood at the sink, her back to me, slicing carrots.

"You're not going to let up on this, are you?"

"You said we would take a nice trip this summer," she said. "You said you would close your office and we would go, just the two of us. So, are we going?"

"You know I can't just close the office and walk out. I'll have to hire someone to run things for me. Answer the phone, manage my accounts."

"You promised."

"All right, Sarah, all right. I'll see what I can do."

Sarah turned from the sink and faced me, a carrot stub in one hand, a paring knife in the other.

"You promised," she said.

"Assuming we ever agree on where to go, what do we do when we get there?"

"I don't know," she said, setting the knife and the carrot on the counter. "What does it matter?"

Sarah moved to the kitchen table and began picking up the colorful maps. She gathered them one by one into a stack and then tapped the edges neat.

"Running away to find what's missing is not the answer, Sarah. It's never that simple."

"Nor is it that complicated," she said, walking out of the kitchen toward the rear of the house. "I just thought it might be something we could do together."

"We can stay home and do that, Sarah," I said. "Shut the doors, pull the drapes. We can stay right here and do that."

Her reply was muffled by the shutting of the bedroom door. The lock being thrown.

FOLLOWING my solitary birthday dinner — peanut butter on rye bread with a medley of sliced carrots — Rusty called to wish me a happy birthday, but after the usual wisecracks about getting old and decrepit, the perfumed cavalier let slip what was really on his mind. It so happens the first payment on the installment plan for adulterous affairs has fallen due. Rusty's new lover (Madeline?) has grown weary of their clandestine encounters and now desires a more conventional relationship. Like other couples, she wants to go out and have a few laughs. Knock back a cold one. In public.

"Well, it was too good to last, Rusty. So now what do you do?"

"Oh, I'm going to take her out," he said. "We have a date for next Thursday."

"Don't be a fool. You know half the people in this town. Where could you possibly go?"

"We're going to Phil Brady's."

"Let me get this straight, Rusty. *You* are taking out a flesh-and-blood woman other than your wife to drink beer at Phil Brady's Bar? Phil Brady's is a place you take your brother-in-law for a game of eight ball."

"We'll be there next Thursday afternoon," he said.

"This seedy date of yours is a bad idea, Rusty. You understand me? You're letting Mr. One-Eye do your thinking for you again. Remember, he has no brains. He cares naught for thought."

"I'm a full-grown man in the prime of my life," he said. "And these days the women look at us. It's true, Gatlin. Walk into a crowded restaurant and watch the women size you up and down. Try it and see. Next time you're out shopping watch the women in the aisle turn to give you the once over. They're out there looking, friend, and taking notes and thinking about us. And I can handle it. I deserve it. I want it."

For a man as big as he is, I couldn't get over how softly Rusty spoke. That or he was trying to keep from being overheard.

"Besides, it's not just sex," he said. "Sex is only part of it."

"That's not what you said yesterday. Yesterday you said it was passion. You said passion was saving your marriage."

"I never said that," he said. "Leave my marriage out of this. Look, this woman enjoys my company. We can be together and just talk. She thinks I'm funny."

"You can't talk to Julie?"

"Sure I can talk to Julie. We've been talking for twenty-five years!"

He's not whispering now.

"But it's different," he said, lowering his voice. "Julie and I have two teenagers. We fall in the bed every night like dead people. There's no time left over."

How much time before Julie learned he was hammering a neighbor lady? Assuming she didn't already know.

"Let me put it this way," Rusty said, "with the girls always under foot, spontaneity in our sex life is out of the question. Besides, Julie's not really keen on spontaneity if you want to know the truth. She likes everything in its place. And she definitely doesn't like me to wake her up for sex."

"What's that leave?"

"Julie's an early morning person. She likes to make love early on a Saturday or Sunday morning while the girls are still sleeping. Before things get too hectic."

"How often does that happen?"

"Every couple of weeks or so."

"Count your blessings, Rusty."

"Deep down it really ticks me off," he said. "Being humored, pandered to like some adolescent boy, some chappie."

"Chappie?"

"I like sex in the afternoon," he said. "The way God intended."

"That's good, Rusty, I like that. *The way God intended*."

"The fact is one of us is always too tired or half-asleep or angry, so we end up missing each other," he said. "There's just no time."

"Still lots of time for your ladyfriend?"

"She's an intelligent woman who enjoys my company," he said. "She's exciting to be with. We can talk. I make her laugh."

"And then there's the sex," I said.

As if things weren't complicated enough, I had to bite my tongue to keep from telling Rusty how I've bumped into his wife Julie not once but twice recently, huddled over lunch with Cyril Newman, recently separated husband of the Lady Madeline. Cyril is a sharp dresser in his early forties who teaches at L.S.U. Julie and Cyril have been conducting test marketing for a coffee shop south of campus. Both of them were quick to assure me the survey took long hours of tedious work, but the two of them seemed to be muddling along just fine. I can't say that I ever remember Julie looking more aglow. She's done something to her hair. For his part, Cyril looked guilty enough to put in the stocks.

"YOU THREW our television set away?" asked Sarah, emerging from the locked bedroom to watch last night's local news.

I had just eaten my forty-seventh birthday dinner — such as it was — alone, and *she* wanted to catch the local news.

"That's right," I said. "I tossed it out."

"You are losing your mind," Sarah said. "I've always been afraid something like this might happen."

She walked into the front room and peeked out the window.

"There's no use looking out there for it, Sarah. Some old coot put the T.V. in his little red wagon and hauled it off as soon as I threw it out."

Sarah looked at me as if I had given the cat away.

"So now what do we do for contact with the outside world?" she asked. "Send up smoke signals?"

"You're the one always complaining about rampant commercialism, the evils of television. Well, I took the monster by the throat and drove him hence."

"You're getting nuttier every day," she said.

"It's gone, Sarah, believe me."

"So what gives you the right?" she said, backing away

from the front window. "Half of every object in this house belongs to me."

"You don't even like television."

"That's not the point, mister. I don't care about the dishwasher either. Does that mean you're hellbent on giving it to the next old bum who staggers down the street? Is the toaster oven next? What are your deep down feelings toward the can opener? What gives you the right?"

LACKING A BETTER PLAN, I phoned Madeline yesterday and recommended a review of her investment program. A sort of gathering of the minds over business matters. She sounded genuinely pleased and expressed an interest in getting together as soon as possible. I suggested I drop by her place this evening, allowing me ample time to return to Baton Rouge from my theatrical obligations at Angola. She went me one better and proposed I stop by around sunset for a drink. A batch of gin gimlets, she said, her specialty.

So it's a date. Thursday (that's today!) for sunset and drinks on the topless (or so rumor has it) patio.

Chapter 5

"WHERE are you calling from?" asks Rick.

"I'm downtown at the office," I reply. "I got up early so I came to work. Just catching up on some filing. Look, can you pick me up here? I've got an appointment later today and I'll need my car."

"No problem," says Rick. "Still raining there?"

"It's stopped for now, but anything could happen. Maybe we should cancel the trip?"

"Not a chance," he says. "The inmates are counting on us. They're looking forward to meeting you."

"Fresh meat for the table."

"Just try to keep your imagination in check," he says. "I'll be at your office at ten o'clock."

"What's the hurry?"

"We've got to work on your costume."

RICK'S STEPSON Matt is hovering before my office window, his outstretched palms smearing the glass. He normally drops by over the noon hour but Thursday is his day off and he shows up first thing this morning, with an appetite. I feed him donuts and coffee.

"Look there," he says. "You see it?"

"Have a seat, Matt. You're blocking the view."

"What is that?"

"Some kind of hawk. A red-tailed hawk, I think."

Matt takes a seat after pulling his chair up closer to the windowsill. He drums the chair arms with his outstretched fingers.

"I've been watching that hawk for days," he says. "He likes to roost in that big cottonwood down there by the base of the bridge, see it? That's where he's headed now. When he gets hungry or bored, he rides the wind currents rising off the river. He's awesome."

"So, you've taken up bird watching?"

"On the river you can see everything," he says. "Watch all the barge traffic, coming and going. Keep an eye on the weather and the docking of the paddle wheel boats. The sunsets are unbelievable."

His own window on the world. What else could he ask for?

"I'll tell you what *I* want," he says, jumping back to his feet. "I want to put my own boat out there in the river. Float myself right down the big screaming middle of it."

Matt stuffs his hands in his pockets and shakes his head.

"All I need is a boat," he says.

"Borrow one," I say. "Half the people in Baton Rouge own a boat of some kind. Ask around, Matt. If you don't have any luck, let me know. I'll help you find one."

"You want to join me?" he says, turning to face me. "You

ever think about sailing off down the Big Muddy? Stop sitting here staring at it and having a real adventure?"

"Oh, I don't know about that. A big thrill for me is getting my tax returns mailed on time."

"You think I'm nuts, don't you?"

"I didn't say that. I think if cruising down the Mississippi River is something you want to do, you ought to do it."

Matt appears to give this notion of a river journey a moment's serious consideration. Then he leaps into the air.

"O.K., O.K., yeah! Let's say I borrow a boat from someone, a big fine boat. One we can live on for two or three days at the time. I'm serious, man. Stock it with fresh water and supplies and set sail for the coast. We can travel during the day and tie up along the banks at night. We'll catch fish out of the river and hunt small game along the banks. It'll be fucking paradise."

Matt stands at the window, looking down onto the river. He seems at once full of wild emotion and at ease with himself.

"So what do we do for fun?" I ask.

"Explore the river," he says, facing me. "Hunt and fish. Make friends with the Indians."

"Indians?"

"There's plenty of Indian spirits still hiding out along the banks of this river, it's just a matter of knowing how and where to look for them," he says, an eerie gleam in his eye.

Is this all good fun for my benefit or am I now guilty of fostering the daydreams of a potential runaway? And at what point did I allow our relationship to reach to this level? What level *is* this?

"So what do you say?" he says, leaning across my

desktop. "You want to float off down the winding big river? Want to make a run for the coast? Have some real fun?"

EVER WONDER what triggers the occurrence of a given memory? Or why one recollection becomes endowed with more brilliance than another?

One of my most vivid memories is of my father floating easily as a cork in the deep end of a neighbor's pool. My sister and I, just small children, are running recklessly around the pool's cement edge, our voices shrieking. It's simply more than we can believe.

"He's floating. He's floating. He's floating!"

This response gives our father great satisfaction. He grins and wiggles all ten of his toes at once.

My father, rest his bones, was a born liar. He lied, exaggerated, told outlandish stories, fantasized, because he found the world too drab and unexciting. He lied because it was fun. When we were young, he told my sister and me dozens of stories about the wild animals — the lions and elephants and zebras, the elands and emus and bandicoots — that had taken up residence in our large, rambling attic. They all had names, winning eccentricities, long wonderful accounts of how they came to live and prosper in our attic. My father's stories always pitted the smaller, more intelligent animals against the larger, more brutish ones. It was a world fraught with peril and fortuity, a place where wit and cunning carried the day.

In the midst of this morning's thunderstorm, I remember sitting beside my father and his friend Duncan Emes in a partially submerged duck blind somewhere in the vast South Louisiana marsh. The three of us in the blind are bitterly cold and a monotonous shower of pellet-sized sleet has been falling since dawn. We sit huddled under our camouflaged ponchos staring at our rubber boots. About our ankles thin sheets of ice keep forming. I am wearing every article of hunting apparel I own, plus my father's new insulated gloves. And I am still freezing. It is now bleak midmorning and we have yet to see anything even resembling a duck. We saw some blackbirds earlier but they were out of range. Our shotguns are now stacked over in a far corner of the blind, bits of ice and sleet pinging off the oiled blue barrels.

Being twelve years of age, I have long since begun to question the wisdom of our coming here or why we stay, though my father and Duncan seem to be making the most of it. Every ten minutes or so one of them passes a pint bottle to me which I, in turn, pass to the other. I was given a capful of this concoction earlier but as I gagged on the burning contents, I am now relegated to merely passing.

"What we need here, gents, is a hot fire," Duncan says, squinting one eye over the unfiltered lit cigarette dangling from his mouth. "My goddamn feet are froze."

"There's six inches of ice and water in the bottom of this blind, Duncan. How do you hope to build a fire?" says my father.

But he should know better. Duncan, albeit a harmless maniac, seldom speaks with idle mind.

"A crackling hot fire is what we need," says Duncan, getting unsteadily to his feet. "A fire is what we're going to get."

In his cumbersome rubber wading boots and hooded

poncho, the short-legged Duncan is reduced to a stooped shuffle, bringing to life the hunchback Quasimodo, banished from his lofty belfry into the flat, saltwater marsh of Cameron Parish.

"A cozy blaze to warm me bones," Duncan says, peering back at me over one humped shoulder.

He staggers out the back of the duck blind and falls face down into the bottom of the twenty-foot aluminum bateau tied behind. In the utter stillness of the marsh, it sounds like a bomb going off.

"You fuck around and sink that boat, Duncan, and we'll spend the rest of the weekend trying to walk out of this marsh," warns my father.

Duncan answers with maniacal hunchback-laughter and begins rummaging through the gear piled in the bottom of the bateau. After a few minutes he comes looming back up into the front of the blind with a galvanized bucket filled with charcoal briquets. Across the bridge of his nose appears a deep bleeding gash.

"Good night, ladies," he says, "I've busted me honker."

"Not a bad idea," says my father, nodding toward the charcoal-filled bucket. "Now how are you going to light it?"

Duncan wipes a gob of blood off the end of his nose, looks hard at it for a second, then pops another lit cigarette into his mouth. He reaches inside his poncho into his bulging canvas coat pocket and retrieves a small canister of lighter fluid.

"With this here," he says. "Whoowee!"

"Just be careful," says my father.

"A hot crackling fire," says Duncan, giving me a wink.

He douses the charcoal with lighter fluid, tosses in a paper match. And presto. A bucket full of burning fire. The three of us sit hunched over the yellow flames, choking smoke and laughing and warming our cold fingers. Father and Duncan pass the pint bottle. A flock of red-winged blackbirds flies warily overhead. The hard grey sleet pummels down.

"It's my goddamn feet that's froze," says Duncan after a time. "If I could just warm my feet."

He lifts one rubber boot over the open mouth of the bucket, dripping water onto the smoking briquets.

"You're dripping on the fire, Duncan."

"My poor cold feet."

Duncan stands, turns his back to the fire and stuffs one boot into the open mouth of the bucket.

"Goddamn it, Duncan! You catch that boot on fire and we'll be forced to shoot your ass."

"Save your ammunition, boys, I'm already froze to death."

Long yellow flames lick the toe, heel and ankle of Duncan's insulated boot. The distinct odor of burning rubber pervades the blind.

"That's enough, Duncan."

"It's just starting to feel good," he says.

But even Duncan hesitates at setting fire to his own foot. Only there's a hitch. Duncan's oversized boot is wedged so tightly in the bucket, it won't come free. When he lifts his foot, the bucket stays attached. Yellow fire dances up and down Duncan's leg. He shakes his foot violently, sending cherry-red briquets flying.

"Get it off! Get it off me!"

"Watch out!" says my father.

Backing into a corner, Duncan takes hold of the duck blind's wooden two-by-four frame and kicks the bucket of fire against the opposite wall of dried brush and palmetto. In one fluid motion my father grabs me, the ammunition and the shotguns and hustles the two of us out the back of the blind and into the bateau.

"Fire in the hole!" Duncan bellows. "Fire!"

Within the space of a minute the entire front of the duck blind is ablaze. A wall of black smoke begins to drift downwind across the barren marsh and out to sea. My father and I float nearby in the bateau, basking in the heat from the surging flames. I start to say something but my father silences me with a wave of his hand. At long last Duncan comes hurtling headfirst out the back of the burning blind into the waist-deep saltwater.

"Pick up that paddle, son," says my father, "and let's go save his sorry ass."

At a quarter till ten, the phone rings.

"Hello?"

"Word on the street is you had a birthday yesterday," says Cliff. "Were you hoping to keep it a secret?"

"It was no secret, Cliff. Just another day in Paradise."

"So how many does that make?"

"Birthdays? Forty-seven."

"Hot damn, son, you're old as yard dirt."

"Is this a friendly call?"

"It's friendly as *hail*," says Cliff, exaggerating his southern accent. "Which reminds me," he says, "I've got a birthday joke for you."

"Look, Cliff, a friend of mine is picking me up any minute now."

"You just listen here," says Cliff. "There's these two middle-aged schoolteachers from Biloxi named Rachel and Charlotte. Neither one of them has ever set foot outside the Mississippi state line, until Charlotte takes a two-week vacation to New York City. By the time she gets back home she's practically aghast."

"Rachel," says Charlotte, "they got all kinds of folks living in New York City. Every color, every stripe and feather and every persuasion that walks the earth. You ought to see it, girl. Why, Rachel, they got men living in New York City who regularly have oral relations with other men!"

"No," says Rachel.

"Yes, they do," says Charlotte. "They call them homosexuals."

"You lie like a dog," says Rachel.

"That's not all," says Charlotte. "They got women living in New York City who regularly have oral relations with other women!"

"No," says Rachel.

"Yes, they do," says Charlotte. "They call them lesbians."

"Kiss my foot," says Rachel.

"That's not all," says Charlotte. "They got men living in New York City who regularly have oral relations with women."

"No," says Rachel.

"Yes, they do," says Charlotte.

"Well, what do you call them?" asks Rachel.

"After I caught my breath," says Charlotte, "I called him precious."

"Where do you get these jokes, Cliff?"

"I keep my ear close to the ground, son. Be surprised what you hear. What you learn."

"What do you hear from your lusty girlfriend? Madame *X*."

"The delectable Madame *X*," Cliff says, "has begun her slow but inevitable retreat. I told you she would."

"She's called the whole thing off? What happened?"

"She didn't call it off," he says. "Not yet anyway. But it has entered her mind."

"How can you tell?"

"Last time I talked to her, she asked about my kids. Can you believe that? We've never spent ten seconds discussing anything and now suddenly she wants to know all about my kids."

"Maybe she likes children?"

"Don't we all?" Cliff says. "I told her how my three kids hate my guts. How they now blame me for the bust-up of our family, their falling school grades, the high cost of living. You name the quandary and the fault is mine."

"They've probably been listening to their mother," I say.

"There's no probably about it, son. Their mother wouldn't spit down my throat if it was on fire. Claims it would be a waste of good spit."

"She's still bitter?"

"Bitter is only a word," Cliff sneers. "What Marian really wants is to run a large vehicle over my dead ass. Then back up and run over my ass again. But there's just no sense in it. I've admitted I was wrong with that young secretary. I was out of bounds and got what I deserved. The biggest problem with Marian and me was we stopped liking each other."

Is Cliff trying to tell me something?

"I liked her once," he says. "There was a time when I couldn't sleep at night unless she was lying right there beside me, touching me. Her body next to mine. In the first five years of our marriage we never spent one night separate and apart. She was the best thing that ever happened to me. But it didn't last. Then I shamed her in front of the whole world and she's never going to forgive me for it. I'll tell you the sad truth — except for the sex, I'm not sure what we ever had in common."

"How was that?"

"The sex?" Cliff asks. "The sex was just this side of berserk. She was like a wild woman. While it lasted. I will give her that."

"But you didn't *like* her?"

"Sex is one thing, son, being married is something else."

BY ELEVEN o'clock, the day is humid and partly cloudy. The earlier rains have ceased. A late-model automobile heads north on U.S. Highway 61 toward the Louisiana State Penitentiary at Angola. Behind the wheel sits a man bearing an uncommon resemblance to Abraham Lincoln. The individual riding shotgun has donned a flowing white beard. His mouse-colored hair has been dusted with white flour to give it a slightly grizzled, omnipotent look. He wears a long white robe and leather sandals upon his blue-veined, middle-aged feet. About his countenance is the stern foreboding of a deity.

"This is insane, Rick. Absolutely and unequivocally insane."

"You look great," he says. "I mean it."

"Did you see the look on the guy's face we just passed?"

"A bumpkin," he says. "Forget about him. We have bigger hills to climb."

Hills indeed. A roomful of Angola's finest sits patiently awaiting our impending arrival. Depository of the most hardened and violent offenders in this state, Angola is the last stop for many of its inmates. Rick informs me that most of the prisoners are basically quiet, embittered men. Often illiterate or nearly so, they are products of neglected, if not abused, childhoods, he says. They lack self-esteem, a sense of purpose, the firsthand experience of human kindness. Historically, they have solved their problems by resorting to crime and violence. Rick claims that nine out of ten of them hate their fathers. Imagine that.

Slay the father, poison the son.

Chapter 6

RICK AND I turn west off U.S. Highway 61 onto the Angola Road, which ultimately will lead us through the rolling hills and forest of West Feliciana Parish up to the black iron gates of the state penitentiary. Allow me to admit to a vague sense of apprehension. A queer sense of upset at the top of my stomach. I have never been behind bars before. My one brush with the law came at age twelve when I was apprehended with three classmates for tossing eggs at the Widow Wagner's house. Extremely old and prone to fits of arm-waving profanity from the stoop of her front porch, Mrs. Wagner proved the perfect foil for our adolescent rage. And we were not the only ones so affected. Everything about the widow, from her blatant madness to her crone-like agedness, seemed to offend everyone, the adults as well. Even my mother, eternal optimist and spokesperson for the meek and downtrodden, was appalled by the widow's public behavior. It was as if this one isolated old woman embodied a painful portent upon which no one wished to dwell.

After my classmates and I were run down and forced to clean up our egg-spattered mess, the bemused coppers allowed us to go free. So today's expedition to Angola will prove to be my first behind-the-scenes look at the criminal justice system.

"Our goal for today," Rick says, "is to provoke discussion, shake them up a little. These men have spent a lifetime brooding over their fathers. All we can hope for is to get them to talk about it."

"You want the inmates to confront their fathers?"

"I want to get them to open up," Rick says. "To talk."

Topping one last steep, heavily wooded rise, Rick guides our vehicle out onto a broad plateau and into full view of the prison. Before I can think of something ironic to say, we have pulled up alongside the main gate guardhouse — a flat-roofed, white-brick, one-room cubical with mirrored windows to prevent anyone from seeing inside.

When Rick attempts to hand over some identification, he is waved off by the slack-gutted guard who approaches our car. His red plastic name tag reads *E. Bickham—Sergeant*.

"Good day to you, Mr. Creel," Bickham says, stooping down beside the driver's side window in order to look past Rick to me.

I would know this man anywhere. A product of his rigorous training, he has affected the strict guidelines for gainful employment as promulgated by Louisiana Law Enforcement: (1) Candidate shall be described as big-boned and burly, with a slight authoritarian paunch — skinny persons need not apply. (2) As regards the general public, candidate shall demonstrate at all times an insulting demeanor, best characterized by a blustering swagger.

"Morning, Sergeant," Rick says, scratching his beard. "We're meeting with the drama group this morning. In the main rec room."

"That a fact?" Bickham says. "Who's this here?"

"A friend of mine," Rick says. "We're putting on a little skit for the inmates."

"I see," Bickham says, beginning his slow saunter round to my side of the car.

As he passes in front of us, he gently glides the tips of all four fingers of his right hand across the flat surface of the polished car hood. It is a simple gesture that is at once unkind, familiar and provocative. It means to say that you have now wandered onto his turf and as such you are *his* guest and you will be allowed to pass on when he has done with you.

Arriving on my side of the car, Sergeant Bickham appears to become engrossed by the presence of my flowing white beard.

"Is that yours?" he asks.

"No . . . well, yes, actually, it's part of my costume. It goes with the gown and the sandals."

"Who you supposed to be?"

"I'm God."

"No shit," Bickham says.

"It's for the skit," Rick says. "We're doing a scene between a father and his son. Something to provoke discussion among the inmates. Remember, Sergeant, we're volunteers, come here of our own free will."

"I see," Bickham says.

He studies the finely dusted nooks and crannies of my face for what seems like a full minute before slowly breaking into a bemused, faintly simian, smile.

"Well now," Bickham says, ducking his head and giving his belly a reassuring rub, "we get all kinds of strange and wonderful folks here at the farm, all kinds, but I can't say I ever remember anybody disguising himself so's he could get *inside*. No, sir."

He stands, steps back from the car and waves to someone behind the mirrored guardhouse window.

"No, sirree," Bickham says, breaking into loud idiotic laughter, "we've never had nobody try to break *in* on us."

The black iron gates begin to slowly open. Rick puts the car back in gear and eases forward. From behind us comes the booming voice of Sergeant Bickham.

"Now we did have a fellah once dress up as a cow but he was trying to get *out*!"

"That bumpkin just made a fool out of me."

"Forget about him," Rick says.

PRIOR TO HIS quitting drinking seven years ago, Rick and I maintained a lofty, if irregular, orbit around the Planet Alcohol. While some men hunt and fish and others play golf or bowl or read or putter round in the yard or watch television, Rick and I worshiped alcohol. We sat out all Friday and Saturday night under the singing yellow moon, and talked and drank whiskey was what we did. Our wives, possessed of weaker stomachs and better judgment, went to bed at a decent hour. There seemed some complex meaning, some deep motive behind all the drink and hurrah that escape me now — the underlying assumption being we might forge a lasting truth. Most of it was drunken tripe.

Our most celebrated binge began innocently one summer evening with a dreamy discussion of the brown-eyed senoritas down Mexico way. By midnight Rick and I had crossed the Texas state line and were within striking distance of Houston. In the back seat were two cases of lukewarm beer, a fifth of bourbon whiskey and numerous bags of assorted party snacks. We possessed no clean underwear, toothbrushes or change of clothes.

Somewhere near Whinny, Texas, we made a detour to the north in order to visit an old friend of Rick's last known to be living in Lufkin. After a brief but fruitless stop there, we drove south for a late night flyby of downtown Huntsville. Then it was back on the road to Houston for sunrise and more gasoline and a pee stop, before cruising over to San Antonio and a stumbling, mid-afternoon tour of the Alamo.

After a couple of quarts of frozen margueritas and tacos and hot sauce, we somehow made it to the border town of Laredo late that night, where we each bought an armful of strawhats and imitation Mexican blankets. Thus armed, we crossed the border into Nuevo Laredo and pulled up to the first cantina in sight where Rick locked the keys in the car. Three hours later we smashed the driver's side window, piled back into the car and abandoned our plans for old Mexico and doe-eyed senoritas who dwelled there. We arrived back in Baton Rouge around noon on Monday. Our wives were speechless.

But not for long.

IN KEEPING with the dominant prison decor, the main recreation building at Angola is a square, windowless, white brick, flat-roofed, two-story structure complete with regulation-grey painted steel doors. Rick and I pull up to the curb out front, gather our costumes and papers and few theatrical props, and prepare to stroll inside. At this point, I think some few words of mutual encouragement, some stirring, if brief, evocation of the dramatic muses might serve us well (a prayer of safekeeping, perhaps, to the gods of low comedy), but Rick seems suddenly withdrawn and distracted, his mind, I suppose, grappling with the events ahead of us. For my part, I must be careful not to slam my flowing white beard in the car door.

Inside, under a profusion of overhead fluorescent lighting, two dozen men in jeans and blue workshirts are seated in a semicircle arrangement of metal folding chairs at one end of the cavernous rec room as if they had nothing better to do than wait for us show up. Which must be precisely the case, though it seems odd to think of these men sitting here silently, waiting, waiting for something, anything I suppose, some diversion from the unqualified hell of their lives. Off to one side, straddling the grey-painted water cooler, stand two khaki-clad prison guards. They all turn as one when Rick and I enter the rec room.

"Morning, gentlemen!" Rick says. "Nice of you to save us a seat."

From the body of prisoners comes a muted chorus of grunts and mutters, a kind of low-level storm rumbling, but no outright belligerence. And then suddenly a surge of activity. Metal chairs are vacated, the inmates filing one by one before me, nodding and shaking my hand with loose-jointed, infirm grips, their spoken names a cacophony of familiar yet uncommon sounds: Germaine, Adrian, Winston, Wallace, Reginald, Ramsy, Russell, Luther, Damien, Daniel, Mason, Lorenzo. . . . The formal, resonant sounds of their names, their deliberate but cordial manners, contrast wildly with their present surroundings. Taken as a whole, their demeanor strikes me as rather businesslike, judicial, as if to acknowledge that we have all been brought to this moment and place in order to work something out among us. Over against the side wall, still astride the water cooler, the two prison guards are showing each other their whistles.

Rick introduces me to the gathering of Angola prisoners as an old friend and amateur performer come to assist in the staging of today's program. The inmates appear to accept this explanation at face value though my odd costume has not gone unnoticed. The fake beard, in particular, has piqued the curiosity of a number of the men. But rather than staring rudely into my face, the inmates tend to angle up on me from the side or rear, hoping, I suppose, to gain some insight into the mechanics of this great flowing monstrosity.

"How come your beard so long?" asks one young man.

"What's that?"

"Your beard. How come it so *long?*"

"Well, you see, I told Rick, begged him not to get carried away, but he figured my character ought to have some feature, some frightful aspect of his physical persona that transcended all the rest. A symbol. Know what I mean?"

"That's cool, man. But how come it so long?"

Another of the Angola inmates, a lanky, long-haired kid who cannot possibly be older than nineteen or twenty, eases up alongside of me and asks for a match.

"Got any fire?" he says, a dirty-blond mane hiding his eyes.

The overture is delivered in a flat, unkind country drawl. I can't decide if the kid's insolent, bashful or just bored to death.

"No, no, I'm sorry," I say, patting my empty pockets. "I don't smoke."

"Don't matter," he says. "Ain't got no cigarettes."

Further conversation, initiated by me, reveals this taciturn country boy to be a native of Livingston Parish, though it hardly comes as a surprise. Only there in those green piney woods and back country roads exists such a thorough melding of ignorance and uncouth sullen pride. I have heard it said the trees that grow in the parched sandy soil are unfit for anything but firewood. Even the women are to be avoided. This gloomy young man, whatever his past surroundings, whatever his differences with the law, must find the stratified, bleak and violent world of the state penitentiary not wholly to his liking.

"You been in long?" I ask, trying to keep our frail dialogue afloat.

"Long enough," the young man replies.

"How much time you got?"

"Won't be long," he says. "Quick as my lawyer makes appeal, I'll get free."

"You're innocent then?"

"I ain't robbed no old lady. She's dreaming."

"But she claims you did?"

"You tell me," he says, looking me squarely in the eye for the first time. "What kind of ignorant asshole would pistol-whip a old woman in broad daylight, then ride off on his bicycle?"

Our young felon, I'm sure, has spent hours, perhaps days, pondering the sheer bafflement this question might arouse in a listener. And I, too, am baffled.

As IF standing around with a roomful of hardened criminals is not distracting enough, my heart has begun slamming away against the inside of my chest. Over the past several years I have become prone to episodes of rapid heartbeat, brought on largely as a result of stress, too much caffeine, and fitful sleep. The Three Sisters, I call them. Question: What do you do after waking ten times every night with raving dreams only to lie there and listen to your heart pound? Answer: You drink a bucketful of black coffee so you can get some work done. Result: By two o'clock in the afternoon your heart is racing and you are too strung out to even think.

But the worst is being panicked and wide awake in the dark of night and thinking *this is fucking IT.* I'm going to die. Not forty years from now in some high-tech nursing home, not next week, not later on tonight. But now. This goddamned instant! The next thundering heartbeat is going to be my last. One loud crash of bone and heart muscle and it's all over. A gasp, a strangled cry, a shot of blinding pain, the first peek at lasting horror, then light's out. Slow fade to black. . . .

The slightly raised wooden platform serving as a stage at one end of the Angola Prison rec room is curtainless and bare, suggesting both everything and nothing, everywhere and nowhere. While Rick (outfitted now in his white gown and sandals and calling to mind — in spite of my stunning case of stage fright — the living image of Abe Lincoln caught sleepwalking) assumes his position downstage near the edge of the platform, I turn and face the seated and hushed prisoners. An assemblage of eager, desperate, glaring faces awaits our message.

How could I possibly have agreed to do this?

"My Son," I say, beginning to walk down the raised wooden platform to where Rick is standing.

"Father," Rick says.

"I sent out scores of messengers, my Son. I posted watch, deployed escorts, sent up a fiery beacon. I searched everywhere."

"Then look no more," Rick says. "Else you uncover more than you seek."

"I want you to be happy here, Son," I say. "I want you to unwind, unburden yourself."

"And lower my guard?" Rick says. "Let bygones be bygones? Is this the good word you bring me?"

"You are my beloved Son. All I desire is your happiness."

"At what price, Father?" Rick says. "What else must I endure on your behalf?"

"I look only to our reunion."

"We're here together now, Father. Let us openly rejoice," Rick says, moving out from under my hand.

"Sarcasm. Sullenness. You've been avoiding me. Why?"

"Avoid you, Father?" he says. "Displease you? Sooner the moon stray from its trusted orbit, the earth pitch on its axis. Sooner a lie become the truth."

"What you are, my Son, who you are, you owe to me."

"I owe you nothing," Rick says. "Understand, old man? I've done your bidding, Father, and now we are square. Even. Finished. Kaput. I owe you nothing."

"Nothing," mumbles one of the blue-shirted prisoners seated in the front row.

The speaker is a broad-shouldered, heavily-muscled inmate whose head is covered by a red bandanna. Half a dozen prisoners shake their heads in unison. The keenness of their response is unsettling and I forget my next line.

Never one to let pass a dramatic opportunity, however, Rick steps down from the platform into the midst of the startled audience. Several of the men actually shrink back in their seats, unused to seeing theatrical characters wandering from the stage.

"So tell me," ad-libs Rick, "you're the one in charge around here, Father, you make all the rules, this is your far-flung operation. Your walls, your high towers. So tell me, what's the going rate for a pound of raw human flesh?"

Every eye and ear of every man in the room is poised, awaiting my reply.

"With bones or without?" I say.

Rick moves among the astonished audience members, their growing agitation now visible.

"So tell me, Father, where were you when I needed you?" he says.

"I am with you always, my Son."

"Talk is cheap, Pop. When I needed you most, when it hurt the most, where were you then?"

"Where?" asks the big man in the red bandanna.

"When I called for you, Father, why didn't you come?" Rick asks.

"Why?" grumbles one of bandanna's cohorts.

Is it my imagination or do several of the inmates appear on the verge of taking the stage? Toward the back of the room, the two khaki-clad prison guards have fanned out in a semicircle, gunslinger-style, their silver whistles ready.

Standing now on one of the metal folding chairs, his arms outstretched, Rick turns to face me, shouting.

"When they drove the iron nails through the palms of my hands, where were you *then?*"

There follows a moment of silence, broken by uproar in the Angola rec room. A shrieking of police whistles, shouts and mutters of disconsolate theater-goers. The prisoners are on their feet, gesturing, milling, seeking guidance, escape, something.

Precisely where Rick wants them.

Part III

Thursday, June 7

Later the Same Day

Chapter 7

Rɪᴄᴋ ᴀɴᴅ I cross the new bridge over Thompson's Creek, leaving the green hills of West Feliciana Parish behind. After this morning's rain, the creek is running fast and clear over its wide sandy bed. The stiff current ripples the water's surface, shattering the bright sunlight into yellow and gold shards. Seven miles downstream the creek will narrow and deepen before emptying into the brown waters of the Mississippi. From there, a man might flee and find free sailing until he reached the Gulf of Mexico.

"You know, Rick, you could have gotten me killed with that little improvisation of yours."

"Aren't you being a little dramatic?"

"Did you see that guy in the red bandanna in the front row? I thought he was going to tear my arms off."

"That's Cedric Collins," Rick says, dismissing my fears. "He just wanted to shake your hand. Did you hear some of the things those men said about their fathers? The skit went beautifully. I couldn't have written the ending any better."

"What was the big idea anyway? I thought we were going to keep the link between father and son tense but friendly, stay in character. What happened to that idea?"

"Things fell right in place," he says. "I hadn't counted on the anxiety generated between your character and mine. I just took the ball and ran with it. Next time we'll know where we're going."

"Next time?"

"Sure. Did you feel the tension in that room?"

"It will be a cold day in hell before I mount those boards again."

"Never say never," Rick says.

As if by prior agreement, Rick and I settle into pensive silence. Angola is back of us now and we are going home. It seems like we've been gone a week. Yet I cannot quit thinking of the community of prisoners impounded there behind the black iron gates of their hilltop fortress. There they sit or sleep or stand for every minute of every hour of every day. And there they will stay.

What did they make of the two of us? Did we bring them any relief?

My father underwent a battery of electroshock treatments over the last five years of his life. I have this mental image of his angular frame being wired and strapped to a table, the touching of electrodes to his temples, a bolt of energy driving bits of memory and the demons that thrived there free of his writhing body. It is a pathetic image, a picture of black depression run amok.

I remember him returning home from the hospital after each of his treatments looking bewitched, as if something dreadful had taken place on the backside of his brain and now escaped him. I couldn't bear to look at him and I couldn't look away. His feeble conduct was that of a wounded animal. It demanded all our attention and offered nothing back.

For a week or so he tottered around the house in his purple robe and slippers, touching the furniture and the photographs. He seemed to be searching for clues. I remember thinking *it's his mind*. It's not like a broken bone that can be mended and fixed, it's not like the time my sister and I had the mumps. It's unspeakable, something children should be sheltered from.

I often daydreamed of rescuing my father, of charging into a den of his masked captors and scattering them. I was always the daring young hero. I never failed to appear in just the nick of time to save him, for my father to look up from his bonds of wire and steel and flash me his big smile.

And then I set him free.

AFTER OUR NEAR theatrical fiasco and the ensuing eruption of pent-up emotions in the Angola rec room, all the blue-shirted felons were assembled into two shuffling columns and escorted back to their dormitories. I followed Rick through a maze of cell blocks and checkpoints into the depths of the prison compound. We were venturing into an area reserved for the most brutal, the most forsaken of the prison population. There were no reading lessons conducted here, no shop or carpentry classes, no discussion groups on how to best deal with rage and violence. Here there were only brightly lighted hallways lined with windowless cramped cells from which emanated — save for the zoo smells of captured animals — few signs of life. The air itself was dank and uncirculated. A place for men to sit quietly alone and observe the backs of their hands — grey-painted anterooms to oblivion.

We were there to see a prisoner who, for reasons not disclosed to me, was rarely allowed out of his kennel-sized cell. I loitered off to one side out-of-sight as Rick stood before this man's cage and carried on a hushed conversation. Due to my position along the wall, I was unable to determine the race or age of the cell's occupant — an ageless, faceless specter consorting with its visitor. The conversation was not a long one. The two simply talked for a few minutes and then joined hands in fellowship. Rick thrust his hands through the bars (I can only presume in order to grasp the inmate's hands in his own) and laughed out loud. I think I was more than concerned by this gesture, alarmed even. I was dismayed. I saw my old friend standing there, unselfconscious, vulnerable, trusting, having possibly placed himself in harm's way, and it made no sense. And I knew that under no circumstances, under no set of events I could envision, for whatever purpose, would I stick my hands through those bars into that man's concrete cage. Never.

But I could admire the effort.

IN THE OPEN fields on either side of the divided highway leading into north Baton Rouge, long white lines of cattle egrets crisscross the sky. A farmer strikes out for the horizon aboard his mammoth green tractor. Brown moo cows stand and chew. The yellow sun is falling down.

"Your work at Angola, Rick, it's a good thing. I'm not saying I can relate to everything you're trying to achieve. I'm not sure I even understand it, but it has a good feel about it. I guess what I'm saying is I admire your commitment."

"Commitment is not the issue," Rick says. "I get more out of it than I put into it. It's individual people that are important. Every person you meet is an opportunity."

"Every other person I meet is a raving lunatic."

"You exaggerate," Rick says.

"Every *third* person I meet is a raving lunatic."

Rick turns his black, glaring eyes to meet mine.

"Stop trying to be clever and do something," he says. "Do anything, but do it now."

Chapter 8

As FATE WOULD have it, I ran into Madeline's estranged husband Cyril at lunch yesterday. I walked uphill from the river into Po' Boy Lloyd's on Florida Street and there he sat as if waiting for me. I had no choice but to accept his invitation to join him for a bite. Just the two of us. How cozy.

Cyril works in the Marketing Department at L.S.U., but often can be found wandering the downtown area where he acts as a consultant to several local banks. His good looks, agile mind and scratch golf game have stood him well here in the state's capital city.

"Hot enough for you?" he said, loosening his tie.

"It's summer in the jungle, Cyril. How are things with you?"

"I've had better days," he said.

As with many middle-aged men recently separated from their wives, Cyril seemed to be enjoying himself less than originally planned. I have observed this is a state of mind that normally sets in about six months after a man walks out on his family. In addition to perceiving a certain inattention on the part of his children during their weekly visits, he begins to surmise that other men — married and unmarried, friend and foe alike — are conspiring to fuck his wife.

"She changed the locks on me," Cyril said.

"Who?"

"Madeline, that's who," he said. "I stopped by the house the other day and she's holed up in there with another man."

"A man?"

"With the goddamn doors locked!"

"Maybe she was just resting."

"This separation was partially my idea," he said, leaning across the table. "Shit. I had no intention of offering up the mother of my children to every horny son-of-a-bitch who takes a notion. Humping the woman in my very own bed. For Christ sake. I've gotten free only to cuckold myself."

Cyril sat there stunned, a scowl painted on his handsome mug.

"She's got all the men in the neighborhood so juiced up they can't see straight," he said. "I drop by to pick up the kids and every swinging dick on the block is standing in my driveway! It's like a pack of hyenas."

I failed to mention his flagrant tryst with Rusty's wife, Julie, or my sunset appointment with Madeline on the topless patio.

I AM THINKING of yesterday's awkward lunch with Cyril when Rick and I spot a lone hitchhiker facing the sporadic northbound traffic just outside Baton Rouge. He stands beside the highway shoulder, his few derelict possessions draped about him: a faded, overstuffed army-issue duffle bag; gallon plastic water jug; well-used walking stick; dusty old coat; dilapidated straw hat. I am reminded of the attorney Biggs and his mighty tumble. Did the loss of his wife demand the rout of his mind? What is he so earnestly searching for? Try to make conversation, offer him any assistance, and he'll take flight down an alleyway.

Beneath the brim of his soiled straw hat, the forlorn hitchhiker — part-man, part-hoodoo — peers back down the highway toward Baton Rouge. He shares with Biggs the same frantic, emaciated look of the insane.

"Now what do you suppose that poor bastard is doing?"

"A man goes on a journey," Rick says.

"I'm serious. How does a man end up on the road with a sack on his back?"

"Maybe he likes to move around," Rick muses. "Maybe he takes pride in his freedom, his wry cunning. Rover, rambler, bedouin. Hungry but unbowed."

"I can't believe that. Only a fool would allow himself to end up standing alone by the highway like that. Old and beat down, without benefit of friends or family. Probably broke. Probably insane."

"Those may be *your* worst fears," Rick says. "They're not necessarily his."

LACK OF CONTACT with immediate family is something I never worry about. My mother will have it no other way. She called me first thing yesterday to wish me a happy birthday. Jolly

Olivia — part of a dying breed. A writer of elementary school textbooks, she still puts in fifty to sixty hours a week, her slight but rugged physique parked before the blinking word processor. She is up half the night working on various projects, proofreading, building a better book. Retirement, she says, is for old people.

And she seems truly perplexed that her only son has turned forty-seven. Let's see, if I'm forty-seven, that makes her . . . She doesn't want to discuss it.

But then, I'm just as uncomfortable with the topic of death as she is. Having a little candid chat with my mother about getting old and dying would prove as impossible, as excruciatingly personal and embarrassing as divulging the passionate details of my infrequent sex life. What Mother and I talk about is the weather.

At least she can still care for herself. Cliff's eighty-two-year-old mother living back home in Mississippi has gone slap-ass crazy. She now refuses to wash or bathe herself. If not constantly guarded, she will strike out down the center of the heavily traveled four-lane highway leading into downtown Vicksburg without so much as a stitch of clothing on her back.

Sarah's father has begun accusing family members of siphoning off the contents of his deodorant bottles. Everywhere he looks, he sees madness and decrepitude.

Yet I have often wondered what it was like for my mother to wake one morning widowed and in debt with two teenage children and a world in turmoil. How did she cope? What wellsprings of strength, character, enabled her to deal with all of that? My mother is a reserved, soft-spoken person. A lady who doesn't hold with a lot of emotional handwringing, fancy speeches or buck-passing. To her way of thinking, a person determines the best course of action available and then does it. It's as simple as that. And things are never as bad as they seem.

I am my father's son.

Chapter 9

As RICK AND I enter the city limits, the phallic-shaped state capitol building looms into view. A crude, if fitting, monument to the cheats and scoundrels who gather within its walls. Out over the Mississippi, a silver jetliner circles, preparing for its long descent into Metro Airport. Sunlight glimmers off the aircraft's polished aluminum sides. On the cement ledge of a railway overpass above the highway some lovesick daredevil has scrawled with red paint the declaration: *Ryan loves Linda 4-ever.*

As if this gesture were not reckless enough — imagine hanging perilously out over the barricade with a bucket of paint and a brush while thirty feet below the four-lane traffic rushes past — Ryan has returned a second time to cross out the name Linda and inscribe with green paint the name Alice: *Ryan loves Alice 4-ever.*

Here is demonstrated not only the lengths to which adoration can drive us, but a striking example (if we are to take Ryan's part) of the resiliency of the human heart. Even in these dead latter days, when smugness reigns and dispassion flowers, love has found a spokesman.

Alice, albeit, had best remain vigilant.

The most popular schoolboy prank in our neighborhood when we were kids was called rolling. Rolling is when you wrap a classmate's (usually female) house and lawn in ream upon ream of pastel-colored toilet paper. Lawns with lots of tall trees produce the most spectacular results — a cascade of pink and blue banners streaming in the early light. The immediate concern is getting our grubby little hands on that much toilet paper. That's where my father comes in.

Father is our bagman. You can imagine the chances of a gang of twelve-year-old boys buying two dozen rolls of toilet paper on a breezy summer's eve without raising eyebrows. People ask questions. They're not as stupid as they look. My father, on the other hand, can walk away with half the stock of toilet paper at the local grocery and no one even winks. One of the bag boys helps him carry it out to the car.

As agreed, father stays home and distracts my mother while my friends and I pull off the job. We hit the ground like crack commandos and in no time it is finished. What only moments before had been a dull suburban lot is suddenly transformed into a papered wonderland! The tall trees on the lawn billow like the creaking sails of Spanish galleons, the flower beds become pink-and-white snowdrifts. The mailbox sports an oversized, gaudy paper bow.

Back safely again at my house, it is pandemonium. Everyone has his story: The toilet roll that gets stuck in the top of the oak tree; the next door neighbor's searchlights; the passing squad car; the one kid who always steps in the dog shit. Father herds us out onto the porch and presses for more details. He wants the cold facts.

The morning after one of these late-night commando raids, my father always finds an excuse to take my friends and me on a slow drive around the neighborhood. Invariably, we pass last night's rolling job.

"Somebody got rolled! Somebody got rolled!" we howl from the backseat.

"Damn fine job, too," my father says.

FROM A SHALLOW DITCH by the roadside a black-spotted puppy trots aimlessly out onto the four-lane highway, heedless of the onrushing traffic. Rick brakes and pulls partway onto the grassy median, just missing him. The dog squats agog on the yellow highway center line, his tongue dangling.

"By the way, Rick, I've been seeing quite a lot of Matt lately."

"That a fact?" he says, not taking his eyes from the road.

"He looks great. I mean it. I've never seen him so enthusiastic, so animated. Huck Finn finds joy on the open river. His whole life is on fire. He mostly wants to talk."

"He should try talking to his mother," Rick says, his hands visibly tightening on the steering wheel. "She's half sick with worry."

"Give him a little room to operate," I say. "He's drawn a line in the dirt and now he feels he can't back away from it. This is his big chance to show how independent he is."

"And drive his mother and me insane?"

"In case you've forgotten, growing up is sometimes painful. For all concerned."

Rick checks the side-view mirror and moves into the one-lane access ramp leading up to the elevated expressway north of downtown.

"Punishing his mother for his problems with me is mean spirited," he says. "It smacks of something his father might have done, provided his father had hung around in the first place."

"Maybe he's fighting with you because you're the closest thing to a father he's ever had."

Rick and I cruise down the expressway above the rooftops past the gritty Exxon refinery — a moonscape of spewing grey towers, smokestacks, huge storage tanks and steel tubing — past the white-columned Governor's mansion and what remains of downtown Baton Rouge before swinging to the southeast where the landscape breaks open onto a panorama of high-rise hotels, posh restaurants and modern office buildings.

"This is not the way to my office, Rick."

"I know," he says. "But I've stumbled across something I think you might appreciate."

"I have an appointment later today."

"It's only five," he says. "You've got to see this."

Rick zooms down the exit ramp at College Drive and heads north past the Webb Park golf course and over to Goodwood. At the corner of Goodwood and Airline Highway we turn left into the front entrance of Woman's Hospital, our final destination, it appears, on this muggy day in June.

The hospital is a large, modern complex set at the intersection of two well-traveled boulevards. From time to time I huddle there with my doctor-clients, all of whom have a penchant for predawn business meetings in the hospital cafeteria. At that quiet hour of the morning, with its many windows darkened, its patients asleep, its red flashing roof and antenna lights, the hospital is a mammoth airship hovering silently over the fog-draped fields. It is hauling its load of sick and dying up and away and out of public view.

But in the full light of day Woman's Hospital looks just like any other group of dull buildings. A structure made of steel and brick and glass where grief and heartache visit regularly, sometimes blindingly, and all too often in front of perfect strangers.

Thursday afternoon must be a popular time for visiting here at the hospital because it takes us ten minutes to find a parking place.

"You said you've discovered something I would appreciate?"

"Keep your shirt on," Rick says. "Follow me."

Rick and I enter the newly renovated hospital lobby and stroll over to the wall of polished steel elevators at the back. Boarding, a green-clad orderly asks us what floor.

"Nursery," Rick says, nodding.

OVER TIME, perhaps as the inexorable consequence of bad memory or the slow process by which loss is reconciled in the aging mind, I have begun to think of Sarah's several miscarried fetuses as one. Or rather as the same life, the same being (use your own word) struggling to be born. I have not discussed this with Sarah. On occasion, in a fit of daydreaming out my office window or awakened by nightmares in the pit of night, I have tried to imagine the existence of the child who was not to be. I have tried to conjure up its looks, its sex, its manner, its way of moving through the world. This kind of speculation, I know in my heart, is not profitable, is clouded by ignorance, fostered by pride. The memory of one who has not lived is grey and shadowy and will not stay still. He is like a scrap of wind. He has no name and no sorrows to tell.

One humid summer night when I was a boy, with my mother asleep beside him, my father aimed the business end of an automatic pistol at the center of his own heart and pulled the trigger. He missed. The small caliber bullet broke the skin's surface, glanced off his rib cage, and tunneled deep into the soft tissue of his left lung. It lay glowing there like an ember. But it did not kill him.

What fears flashed through my mother's mind as she snapped awake in the dark bedroom, the concussion of the pistol shot still ringing in her ears? Did she hesitate before switching on the light?

No one, not one member of his family, not a single friend or hunting buddy admits suspecting my father was so distraught, so perilously near the edge. No one, apparently, ever contemplated his ordering a handgun from the back pages of a magazine and using it on himself. Suicide was unseemly. It put an ugly crack in the turning world.

His motive for trying to kill himself, his reason for bringing violence into all of our lives, was never revealed. He left no note, no explanation, no list of grievances, no message of farewell. It was as if he had nothing left to say. No words to leave us.

My sister and I spent the remainder of that summer with our mother's parents on their small farm in East Texas. We rode the old mare until she balked, chased the chickens, and terrorized the milk cow, while inside the old couple cooked hams and pot roasts, served up plates of cornbread and biscuits and fresh vegetables, plied us with cookies and ice cream and fruit pies. Our father was very sick, they explained. My sister and I nodded our heads gravely and then ran outside to play Indians in the barn.

When we returned home in September, we found our father looking pale and thin but overjoyed to see us. He said he had contracted a bad case of gorilla fever and gone temporarily out of his head. He smiled and said it would not happen again.

For some months after, father rode a long, uninterrupted wave of well-being. He coaxed my mother into taking us to the Ozark Mountains in the fall to see the leaves change. At Christmas he outdid himself. He single-handedly wrapped the outside of the house with myriad strings of blinking colored lights. He belted out Christmas carols from dawn till dusk; he built such infernos in the den fireplace that it drove the entire family out into the backyard to cool down. He sat on the floor and beat my sister and me at our new Christmas games.

ARRIVING at the second floor of the Woman's Hospital, Rick and I exit the elevator and follow the bright blue arrows to the rear of the building. Our goal, however, is not the well-lighted nursery with its fat sleeping newborns and groups of proud dads and grandparents cooing and shooting film through the glass partition. Our purpose, it seems, lies elsewhere. Rick motions to one of the attending nurses and we are admitted through a locked door into a short hallway.

"Where are we?"

"Hold your horses," Rick says.

At the end of the hall, through another door and past a nurse's station, we enter a small, windowless room whose walls are lined with plexiglass incubators — small self-contained space stations for travelers not fully adapted to Planet Earth. Inside four of the incubators are living creatures. I say creatures because at first glance they more closely resemble small animals or birds than human beings, their very existence seeming so tenuous and remote, even questionable. I could hold any one of them in the palm of my open hand, though the thought of disturbing them is unbearable. I am almost nauseous with the sensation of remorse, yet in the same instant, I feel wonder.

"Relax," Rick says. "You look like you're about to faint."

"I'm all right."

"Look at this one," he says, tapping gently on the side of one of the plexiglass containers. "Look at him, will you."

Inside the incubator the skin-and-bone spacebeing is lying on his back, his legs drawn frog-like up along his sides. His head and eyes are wrapped in layers of white cotton gauze. A single clear tube runs up one nostril and four wired monitors are taped to the skin of his chest and abdomen. An IV is inserted in his scalp. As if acknowledging our shuffling presence, he stretches one tiny splayed hand toward the ceiling, waving violently.

"What's wrong with him, Rick? Why is he trembling so much?"

"Cocaine addiction. All the babies in this room are born of addicts. Cocaine, heroin, alcohol abuse, you name it. Most of them have been orphaned."

"Jesus."

"This is what I was telling you about," he says.

For some reason, both of us are practically whispering, putting our heads together to talk.

"I don't get it," I say.

"Take a good look at this one," Rick says, bending down beside the trembling cocaine addict. "Come here and look closer. Concentrate on him. Look at his hands. Study his little feet and toes. Look at those ears, will you. Check out that perfect set of fingernails."

"Will he live?"

Rick leans forward and takes a quick look at the index card affixed to one side of the incubator.

"His name is Jason," he says. "And I'll make a small wager with you. Commit yourself to spending twenty minutes a day for the next seven days observing this child. Touch him. Stroke his aching bones. Talk to him. If the medical staff will allow it, hold him. Watch his struggle to be. If at the end of one week you are not deeply concerned about Jason's immediate future, if you don't have a better understanding of what matters, then it won't take a trained physician to determine which of you two is the more ill."

* * *

ON MY EARLY DRIVE to work this morning, I crossed paths with the unknown runner. Almost daily, in the teeth of every season, I will meet up with this resolute soul. Gaunt, with vacant stare and telltale loping gate, he embodies the stern, self-crucified visage of the daily jogger. Is it the rapture that drives him so? Or agony at the body's creeping demise? For my part, he can have it. One lap around the block and I'm crippled for a week. My knees lack all vestige of internal cushioning, resulting in a slow but continuous pounding of bone upon bone. I am prone to shin-splints and lower-back pain. I have weak ankles.

A weakening of strength, Sarah said yesterday, *threatens your identity.*

It takes me minutes to empty my bladder.

"What you need, mister, is a good doctor," Sarah informed me late last night.

"I never felt better in my life," I said.

"Let's face this together, dear," she said, smiling in spite of her solemn tone, "there's something terribly wrong with your insides."

"There's nothing wrong with my insides."

"You've been eating peanuts again, haven't you?" she said. "I can always tell."

"What makes you —"

"Don't try to deny it," she said.

Flatulence and rounding the good horn of forty-seven. Some menacing, as-yet-unidentified, internal male organ is roused, awakened from its youthful slumbers, effecting a nominal but continuous drip of noxious chemicals. There is by consequence an ominous gathering of great gases, a colossal wind redolent of bear or goat — at once gangrenous, corrupt, prodigious and wild. The very air itself seems foul and unbreathable, *a huge and rotting human fungus,* a dense and untreated roiling black sewer.

"Come over here, Sarah, and lets have a little birthday hug. What do you say? Just a hug."

"Don't get your hopes up," she said, vigorously brushing her black hair. "I'm still perturbed with you."

"All fun aside now," I said. "It's my birthday. There's no sense the two of us getting locked into a protracted battle over this vacation thing."

"Think of it as a kind of training exercise," she said. "While I'm traveling out west this summer, your mind will already be hardened to the idea."

"It's not my hardened mind that concerns me."

Part IV

Thursday, June 7

Late Afternoon

Chapter 10

SEVERAL YEARS AGO my mother sent me the last of my father's personal possessions. Included in the booty were his high school and college annuals, a number of old letters, his Navy discharge, a sketch pad, some black-and-white photographs of my father as a young boy, and various documents and odds and ends. Near the bottom of the box, in an old spiral notebook, I found rough copies of his stories. There were only three dozen or so, all written in his cramped handwriting on cheap, yellowed paper and many of them were unfinished, several of them mere fragments. But I was astonished. Here in my father's own hand were the earliest heros and heroines and villains of my childhood — the forces of good and evil made manifest so that even a child could know and applaud the difference. Characters whose names and deeds had shaped my imagination, if not my young character. They were awkard, unpolished stories, but they staggered me. I couldn't have been more moved if my father had walked into the room where I was sitting.

My father could paint with brush and oils, handcarve wooden animal figures of intricate shape and design, recite whole poems from memory, compose delightful stories off the top of his head. If required, he could disassemble an automobile engine into eight thousand separate tiny pieces and then put it all back together again. He was an outdoors man. He was one of the most innately talented persons I have ever known. He was a man of extremes. He was either nine miles high or stuck flat on the bottom. His bouts of wordy rapture often ended in episodes of speechless terror. He could keep a roomful of people on the edge of their seats listening to his stories or go for days without speaking. He was the victim of his own grim moodiness. When all else failed, when things got as bad as they could get, he took to his room.

What happened then was a kind of siege, one that might last for days. My sister and I concocted stories about the mad man living behind the bedroom door. The wild-eyed hysteric who groaned and wept and pulled the pictures from the wall. The creature who bloodied himself, the naked lost soul who looked into the faces of his own children and did not know them.

I HAVE this recurring dream. I'm standing in my darkened living room. Hovering in the shadows outside the front window is a hooded figure. It's my father. The figure motions for me to open the window and allow it to come inside. Whatever the spirit wants, whatever it needs, is in here with me. Sensing my reluctance to open up, the hooded figure begins tapping repeatedly on the window glass — the fierce, insistent, staccato rapping of bare bone on brittle glass. If the glass should break, I am certain I will die.

And the house is jammed with people. In my dream I'm having a party. Everyone attending is laughing and drinking, conversing in small groups. I hold a blue-eyed child on my lap and try to make him smile. Then the hooded figure taps and the scene changes. Suddenly all my guests are dead, part-dead, part-living. I look to save the child, but the child is one of them.

Then the dream collapses into the day of my father's funeral. I am hastily packing a suitcase with a black suit, black shoes, white shirt, somber tie. My wife Sarah, inexplicably, is there at my side, offering her support, as are a few sympathetic friends. I am glad to see the end of my father's suffering — the raving psycho is finally free to rest.

Suddenly there is a telephone call. On the other end of the line a male voice informs me that my mother has been involved in a terrible car crash. She was killed instantly. I am stunned, anguished. How can this be! How can anyone lose both parents in one day to unrelated causes? It's not sensible.

I am not prepared for this.

And then in a flash of scene changes, Sarah and I are face to face in a hushed room, alone. We are no longer the spry, suntanned young people we were moments before but rather the serious middle-aged couple we have become. There is so much I need to do. Sarah smiles up at me, her blue eyes wide and flashing, about to speak. She is with child. Goddamn. I'm too old! I'll be a broken-down old man before the baby is grown. How did this happen?

I am not prepared for this.

* * *

RICK PULLS the car up to the curb in front of my office building and kills the engine. After six o'clock on a Thursday evening, much of downtown Baton Rouge is already locked up and deserted, the drafty streets a vacant metaphor of small town America. One of the few persons still out and about is our man Biggs, Third Street's designated spook. Biggs is fishing through a sidewalk trash bin that opens from the top. The old boy takes his sweet time, thoroughly inspecting each paper bag and cardboard box, perusing the occasional bit of junk mail. What we have here is the specialist, a roving connoisseur of the detritus left behind by the rest of us. Another despondent male citizen trying to keep body and soul together.

Are we all a mere six months away from living out of trash cans?

Biggs puts an empty drink can into each of his coat pockets, hikes his pants up over his protruding hipbones and sets sail down the avenue in search of more treasure. No rest for the weary.

"What are your plans for Saturday afternoon?" Rick asks.

He lifts his chin and scratches the whiskers along his throat.

"Nothing much," I say. "A little rest and relaxation. Sarah and I plan to spend the whole day together. I'm cooking gumbo."

"Sounds like fun," Rick says. "Tell you what, Gatlin. Put the gumbo on to simmer and come check out the five o'clock program at the center. And bring Sarah. I've got a Thai dance group from L.S.U. scheduled to perform traditional dances.

They've got a ceremony honoring the sun that will knock your socks off."

"I'll mention it to Sarah."

As I move to get out of the car, Rick puts a hand on my shoulder and stops me.

"I appreciate your help with the skit," he says. "I mean it. I've been trying for weeks to make some kind of breakthrough with the prisoners. Today we hit a home run."

I open my door but Rick stops me again.

"About visiting the boy Jason at the hospital," he says. "I'll make a couple of phone calls and set it up so you can stop by anytime you like."

In the street below my open door a gust of wind blows a caravan of tumbling gum wrappers along the curb.

"So what do you say?" he says.

"Tell me, Rick, on your triumphant march across the planet, do you ever stop and consider anyone else? Have you wondered how difficult it might be for the rest of us just to crawl out of bed and be civil?"

"And your point is?" he says.

"You must know how painful visiting that child might be for me, don't you? Do you?"

Rick shrugs his shoulders and smiles.

"I was only thinking how good it might be for Jason," he says. "And do me another favor will you?"

"What now?"

"Next time you talk to Matt, tell him to call his mother."

Out on the river a tugboat sounds a terrific blast of its foghorn, causing a white speckled pigeon to explode from his perch on a building ledge into the pastel sky above our heads.

He pitches wing-to-wing down the high-walled, narrow street.

"Matt is a friend of mine," I say. "I'm not taking sides."
I move to get out of the car but Rick stops me again.
"Are you all right?" he says.
"I feel fine. Everything's perfectly fine."

UPSTAIRS in the warm hush of my office suite, I am surrounded by the familiar sight of leather furniture, polished oak bookcases and the perpetual fireworks show on the blank screen of my on-line computer. Everything in its proper place, every brochure and prospectus on hand, every pencil and paper clip ready for business. (Failing all else, oh merciful, implacable God our Father and Provider, let there be a profit.)

What possesses a man to sit staring out his office window onto the surging brown river beyond? What's so compelling about birds and trees and running water? How does all this watching accrue to my benefit? When I finally see what I'm looking for, will I recognize it?

Outside my window the sun has swollen to twice its normal size as it sinks toward the green treetops. Looking south toward the L.S.U. campus, the surface of University Lake has become a brilliant pool of reflecting fire. Atop the flames, cormorants, snowy egrets and all manner of waterfowl are circling their roosts. In the old neighborhoods beneath the towering trees, the first lights are appearing in windows and porches. It's early evening in the rain forest.

Down in the church playground opposite my building, a stray dog urinates against a swing set.

They *are* taking over. The other night I watched a pack of seven mongrels parade leisurely across my front yard, digging, defecating their large, brown piles. They smelled each other's steaming waste, they flapped their pink, lolling tongues.

After defiling my lawn, they hit the neighbor's trash cans, exploding chicken and steak bones up and down the sidewalk. Tissues and bits of soiled paper were scattered over the grass and into the street. In the driveway lay a partially eaten, disposable diaper.

It had to be stopped.

When was it? Five nights ago? Six? I was startled by the clatter of a trash can lid hitting the hard surface of the street. Here was my chance. On my way through the kitchen I grabbed a barbecue fork and eased out the back door. From out in front came the sound of a trash can tipping over and a bottle bursting against the curb.

Sons of bitches.

I sneaked down my neighbor's hedgerow until I neared the trash cans by the street. At that hour, the road's asphalt surface looked as clean and smooth as a piece of slate. I was so close to the animals I could hear them gumming my neighbor's garbage. I crashed through the hedgerow and drove the nearest animal into the street. Turning, I dove headlong for a second one but missed. I now lay face to face with a third mutt that just stood there chomping his bit of refuse like a mechanical toy. I spat into his open, incredulous mouth, and he tore off in panic down the street.

I remember rolling over onto my back and looking up at the night sky. The moon was high overhead and waxing. I wondered if Sarah was aware of the scavengers. She had never said a word about them to me. Never complained, never mentioned them. She could sleep through anything.

And what made this quiet neighborhood so special I wanted to know? What was the singular attraction? Did I have to start guarding my own garbage? Throw up a barricade around my life and property? Where might that kind of madness lead?

Chapter 11

THE VIEW out my office window, this high-flying lookout post suspended over lush gardens and surging big river, is mine. The sinking yellow sun, the green leaves on the trees, the birds in the air, all belong to me. I am lord of the southern rain forest. A fool in his rented fortress — home of sailing clouds and sweeping vista. Take a long look.

The pale early dawn is the most serene time here in my steeple. Snatches of ground fog slip across the river's flat surface, the trees and foliage drip with heavy dew. The levee is blue-shaded and cool. Last night's yellow moon still shines brightly. And the whole humid day lies ahead.

Gliding by me in the day or night are the tankers and cargo vessels. Big ocean ships with bright flags and exotic sounding names. Great cities of steel and flashing lights. Long after they pass, their wakes will crash like echoes at the levee's edge.

Every evening there is the sunset. A great Jupiter fireball of heat and light dropping slowly into the haze, the western sky over Texas turning to yellow and gold. The earth is inflamed. I am never prepared for such a sight. I sit bug-eyed in my leather armchair and promise this time never to forget.

FROM OUT IN THE HALL comes the clomping of heavy shoes that fall silent before my office door. A visitor? Glowering janitor making his evening trash rounds? Irate investor come to settle accounts? The door swings open and in leaps Matt.

"Holy shit, I've got it!"

"Have a seat, Matt. Got what?"

Matt takes a seat on the edge of an armchair. Both his hands and feet are moving.

"I've got a boat!" he says. "Seventeen-foot Mohawk canoe, life jackets and paddles. Practically brand new."

"You're kidding!"

"It's got a fiberglass hull and plenty of room for two men and storage. It's awesome. You've got to see it. I'm taking it out for a test run on the river this Saturday. You interested?"

"This Saturday? I've got plans for Saturday. Sarah and I are cooking —"

"I told the owner I had an adult going with me," he says. "It made him feel better. So will you come?"

"If I had known ahead of time, I —"

"You ought to see it out there," Matt says, hopping up from his seat. "If you went out there just once, one time, you would see. You don't have to be afraid of the river just because everybody else is."

"Who said anything about being afraid?" I say. "Cautious perhaps. I mean, Jesus, Matt. A canoe? The river is over a hundred feet deep in places. What if you tipped over?"

"We're not going to tip over," he says. "We're going to float on top of the water. In the canoe."

His confidence is assuring.

"The river is not the enemy," he says, moving to the window. "Not to me. It's just big, big and wide and flat, like a big swollen brown lake, only it's alive and moving. You don't know where you're going and it doesn't matter where you've been."

"Sounds like middle age."

Matt turns his back on me and points a finger at the southern horizon.

"You're out there free on the river and everything is alive and moving, drifting round the next bend, down the river and out to sea. And you go with it," he says. "So what do you say? Will you go?"

Matt turns and faces me, almost angry now.

"We're never going to get out on the Mississippi if we stand around waiting for somebody to come along and take us. I've got the canoe. There's the river. If we don't go now, we may never forgive ourselves. Never. Besides," he says, looking down at his boots. "You're the only one I know to ask."

"If I had known about this a couple of days ago, maybe. . . ."

"Sure," he says.

Matt drops back into the leather armchair, his floppy flannel shirt slowly settling around him like a collapsed circus tent. There is no joy in River City.

Maybe I can fix it.

"I tell you what, Matt. Let me talk to Sarah about Saturday."

"Goddamn terrific," he says, up and dancing back to the window. "We can put in at the foot of the new bridge and float down to the island."

"What island is that?"

"There's an island sitting in the middle of the river. Just above the ferry landing at White Castle. Off Plaquemine Point. The island can be our base camp. From there we can explore the whole river, up and down."

Matt has begun leaping off the carpeted floor.

"Let's just take this one step at a time," I say.

"Sure, sure, that's fine. Fucking fantastic! You're never going to regret this, as long as you live," he says, spinning in mid air and then rushing for the door.

"Hold up a second, will you?"

Matt stops and turns, continuing to hop in place.

"Yes?"

"Tell me, have you spoken with your mother lately?"

MATT IS no sooner out the door and down the hall than the phone rings.

"Hello?"

"Is this what happens when you get old?" Cliff asks. "I mean, does life become one long stretch of suffering work without joy or poontang? And then you die?"

"No, Cliff. Age has nothing to do with it."

"Forty-seven is old I'm here to tell you. I've never had a forty-seven-year-old friend before. What's it like, Gatlin?"

"Once you get used to the aluminum walker, it's swell. By the way, seen anything of your lusty girlfriend?"

"I stopped by her place last night," he says, "only this time there was no discussing my kids. No talk of former wives or husbands. About the future or the past."

"What are you saying?"

"I screamed and rolled over and died and went to heaven," he says.

"When was this?"

"Last night. All night. This country boy rode the slow train to heaven. And God was wearing high heels. Buck naked in a pair of alligator high heels. She wouldn't take them off. Like to ruined me."

"What's it like fucking with shoes on?"

"I died and went to heaven," Cliff says.

"You're saying she likes the kinky stuff?"

"I never said that," he says. "What she likes is gentle persuasion. To be sought after, pursued and then caught. It's a little game we play."

"She pretends she doesn't want it? "

"The first time she says no," Cliff says, "she means yes."

THE FIRST TIME Sarah told me *no*, she meant if I didn't keep my filthy hands to myself, she was going to scream. She meant if I didn't stop immediately, I would be having intercourse with myself for the next six weeks. When she said *no*, she meant fold up your tent poles, lover boy, and move on.

Here are the selected highlights of a conversation that took place earlier this week:

"The last time was Saturday morning, Sarah. Three days ago."

"You act like it's been weeks," she said, not bothering to look up from her book.

"Count them, Sarah. Saturday, Sunday, Monday. Three days."

"You're counting the days all wrong. You always exaggerate."

"I can grow a beard in three days. I can walk from here to New Orleans in three days. My eyeballs are about to pop out of my skull."

Having opened Pandora's box, I had no one to blame but myself.

"Do you really believe that kind of talk is going to somehow entice me to make love to you?" she said, setting her book aside. "Do you think that's stimulating? Is that what you think? A little romance, Gatlin, a little human tenderness, would serve you a lot better."

"O.K., Sarah, I'm sorry. I was just kidding."

"What's happening to you?" she said, her blue eyes watering. "You weren't always like this. You used to be the most romantic, most thoughtful person I've ever known. You used to write me little poems, remember? Bring me roses and little gifts whenever you went out of town. When was the last time you wrote me a poem?"

My father occasionally spoke to me of how poetry, a memorable story, the well-turned anecdote or phrase, or just good writing, all held a kind of primacy over our corporeal lives. Words, he liked to say, are what we leave behind.

And to illustrate his point, to wipe the smiles from cynical faces, he had only to summon up the vision of his own grandfather, his mother's father. Grandfather Stewart, whom I never met, was described as a reserved man who never left the shade of his front porch without his hound dog or his cowboy hat. He had a drooping, snow-white mustache that was stained at the edges from a lifetime of coffee drinking. He could recite every word, verse, and chapter of the Bible, and loved small children above all things. He had luminous, sky-blue colored eyes and was blind. And he had the power to heal. Grandfather Stewart could pass his hand over a burn or minor injury, mumble a prayer or magic spell, and stop the pain. Anytime someone in the family or on a surrounding farm was burned or hurt, he was brought to Grandfather Stewart and he would heal him. His words would stop the pain.

My father was a healer, too. He could put his hands near a scrape or a small cut and chase the pain away. You simply had to believe him. As young children, my sister and I believed his every word.

"Stop crying now. Stop I said. Show me where it hurts. There?"

"Yes!"

"Hush now. Stop crying. Be still."

My father cups his big hands together and places them just above my knee.

"Watch the blue spark in the center of my hand," he says. "Do you see it?"

"Yes."

"Watch the blue spark. If you watch the blue spark, the pain will disappear. Do you see it?"

"Yes."

"Believe it. If you believe it, the pain will stop. Do you love me?"

"Yes."

"Watch the blue spark."

Like many marvels of childhood, the blue spark was something that once believed was easily seen. I can still see it.

But sometimes I remember the bad. I recall once finding a fifth of whiskey hidden in the garage and pouring it down the kitchen sink. Father stands there behind me, drunk, his unkept, lunatic's hair flying.

"You prick," he says. "You sneaky, smug, stupid, little prick."

I empty the bottle, cap it, throw it in the trash, and go to my room. I have a book report to write. I feel like a smug, little prick.

IT'S BEEN ALMOST twenty-four hours since I last spoke to Rusty, the fragrant giant, so I'm not surprised when my office phone rings in its cradle.

"Hello?"

"I'm in love," Rusty says.

"Come again?"

"The flowers are blooming, the bees are buzzing. I think I'm in love."

"Excuse me, Rusty, I didn't sleep well last night and it's been a long day. You're what?"

"In love," he says. "Infatuated. Bonkers. Smitten. Call it what you want. I think it's love."

"Sounds like the galloping dumb ass to me, Rusty. Often caused by using your genitals to think with. Take my advice, old friend, zip up and wise up."

"No use being insulting, Gatlin," he says. "My relationship with this woman takes place entirely in the present. Now. This instant. It's like hunger. I can smell it. I want to take a big bite out of her, I want to taste her crack. I want to hold her, touch her, day and night."

"What part of your anatomy is talking now?"

"I didn't mean to fall in love," he says.

"Love? Love! You can't afford love, Rusty. You've got children and outstanding debt. And college tuition to pay for next year. And a wife, for Christ sake. You and Julie have been married twenty-five years. What about that?"

Is vigorous sex with a strange woman the cause or the result of confusion in the master bedroom? Do married people just get tired of screwing each other or is it the constant onslaught of jobs, money, stress and fading youth getting in the way?

"A person can't help what he feels," Rusty says.

"A person can't help being run down by a truck," I say. "A person can't help being born with a clubfoot. Love is something we do. It's voluntary. We make choices."

"I've never felt so good," he says.

"Listen to me, Rusty, if this woman decides to call it quits, you're going to be left out in the cold. You could end up losing Julie and the kids and have nothing to show for it but an arrow in your gut."

"Some men like to ride the merry-go-round, some men like to ride the roller coaster," he says. "My life with Julie is like a piece of old family furniture. It's comfortable, durable and nobody else wants it."

THE GOLD GLARING SUN lights the western sky. The earth seems to pause, shuddering on its tilted axis, before resuming a slow rotation. Bright copper rays make paper lanterns of the magnolia leaves at the top of the tree outside my office window. The nation of birds begins to gather before the approaching sunset, materializing like dozens of hand puppets. Big pompous blue jays and sparrows mostly. Except there. There a lusty cardinal struts, admiring his reflection in the polished glass of my office window. He loves himself. In the branches of the pecan tree, two mockingbirds crack the early evening calm. Out beyond the trees, behind the stout levee walls, the cold running river washes down to the gulf.

"Hello?"

"Sarah, I've been thinking."

"I thought you went with Rick to Angola?"

"I did. We did. I'm at the office. I'll tell you about it later. Let me tell you what I'm thinking."

"Are you all right?"

"I'm fine, listen to me. I've agreed to go on a canoe trip down the river with Matt this Saturday morning. I told him you and I already had plans but if it's all right with you, we'll cook the gumbo on Sunday. Okay with you?"

"What river?"

"The Mississippi River, Sarah. How many rivers do we have in this town? Why don't you come with us?"

"I get sick on boats."

"It's not a boat, it's a canoe. It'll be an adventure. Matt says there's an island we can visit."

"An adventure for you, maybe," she says. "I get weak just thinking about it."

"A real adventure, Sarah, right here in our own backyard. We walk over the levee and down to the river and there we are. We push off and we go. Anything could happen."

"Boats are not my idea of fun," she says. "Besides, I cannot think of a better place to drown."

She's got no problem striking out for the great wild west with no formal plans or destination but a canoe ride down the Mississippi sounds reckless, foolhardy.

So what can we do together? Answer: Bicker and eat.

The other night Sarah and I were feasting on trout — speckled trout fresh from the Gulf of Mexico, lightly battered and panfried to a golden brown — when Sarah looked up suddenly and clutched her throat.

"Sarah? You all right? Say something."

Sarah gave me a wide, blank, blue-eyed glare but said nothing. With her free hand she motioned to her throat.

"Something's wrong with your throat?"

This observation, however astute, only served to agitate her further. This became apparent when she stamped both feet loudly on the floor and sailed her dinner roll just over my head where it ricocheted off the front of the fridge. Collecting herself, Sarah pointed first to the half-eaten trout on her plate and then to the center of her lovely throat. Her expression was becoming slightly more desperate.

"You've got a bone in your throat."

Bingo. Sarah nodded her head frantically but did not speak.

"Eat some bread," I suggested, setting my roll onto her plate.

Instead she placed a hand palm down on each side of her plate and began pounding the table top. This was getting serious.

"Eat a piece of bread, Sarah. Do it now."

Halfheartedly, as much to demonstrate what a complete nincompoop she had for a husband, Sarah tore off a piece of roll about the size of a blueberry, chewed it for what seemed like two minutes, then swallowed.

"Try another bite. A bigger one."

Becoming instantly calm, her sole focus in life being to survive in order to get even, Sarah ripped the dinner roll in half, put it in her mouth and chewed it six or seven times before swallowing. After about a minute she blinked, sat back in her chair and smiled.

"It's gone?" I asked. "You're all right now?"

"It worked," she said. "It's gone."

"That's good," I said, retrieving my fork from the floor where I had dropped it in the midst of all the excitement. "And now may I point out that it has long been customary for the damsel, once saved from her distress, to grant her rescuer intimate, that's not to exclude sexual, favors."

"I'd rather hump the dragon," Sarah said.

She pulled her chair back up to the table, speared another piece of fried trout and ate.

So much for chivalry.

But the one thought that got to me about the fish-bone

episode, if only for the few seconds she sat there grimacing with the small bone lodged in her throat, was of something dreadful happening to Sarah. If I were ever to lose her, let's say, what would happen to me? How far would I fall?

I would under no circumstances portray one of those tanned and perfumed middle-agers with a flashy car and a bleached blonde half his age by his side. When they're not doing it, what do middle-aged men and young bleached blondes talk about anyway? Some of my friends have daughters who are bleached blondes. I don't want to talk about it.

Then again, what if Sarah took a lover? Why not? She's an attractive, quick-witted woman who, when the mood is upon her, is quite capable of extraordinary heights of whopping passion. She could have any man she wished. What if she wished? What if she sat me down one evening, poured out two glasses of good scotch and dropped the big one.

"O.K., dear, please, I want you to understand that I've tried, I've tried so very hard. . . . But there's no use hiding it any longer. It's not fair to you. To us. Don't ask me where or when, but I've met another man. He's rich and good-looking. He sets me on fire."

"He sets you on fire!"

"We've been seeing each other for a year now."

"He sets you on fire?"

"Oh, dear, I'm so sorry, it's all so vulgar, so, so —"

Good Christ, stop the movie. I can't bear it.

A LONE CROW has begun appearing on the window ledge of my office building. He arrived just now — a big, black, sleek bastard with sly beak and piercing cry. He roams up and down the cement ledge like some kind of strutting apparition. Some black-clad arbiter of all that happens below. And he's got his rolling evil eye on me.

Why am I so nervous? My normally dry hands have grown clammy and my contrary heart has begun to tumble. In the deep silence of this office, my ears are ringing like wind chimes. When did I last have something to eat? I feel flushed. Anxious. Perhaps I should phone Madeline and plead fatigue and a long day and postpone our evening rendezvous? Put this whole rotten business out of my mind. Be done with it.

Instead I reach into the top drawer of my oversized desk to retrieve a newly purchased, foil-wrapped condom. I tuck it into a corner of my briefcase beneath Madeline's investment file.

Chapter 12

IT IS a short drive from downtown Baton Rouge over to Highland Road and out to Kenilworth subdivision where Madeline makes her residence. After passing through the absurd brick towers defending the subdivision's entrance (a bit of Olde England removed to sultry Baton Rouge), I take my first right, my second left, and midway down the block turn into a circular driveway before a partially shaded, white brick house. Rather than ring the front doorbell like a stranger to the neighborhood, I walk down the drive running alongside the house and enter the back gate.

"Hello. Anybody home? It's me, your friendly financial planner."

Not a soul. An empty wooden patio bedecked with hanging ferns and potted plants and the faint sound of jazz playing from somewhere inside the house. Now what?

"Welcome, Gatlin," says a voice from behind a wooden lattice partition dividing the deck in two, one side open and filled with plants, the other shaded and cool. "Come sit awhile and rest your bones."

It's Madeline. And looking, now that she emerges from the darkened alcove, more tanned and fit than I remember. Her black slacks and sleeveless yellow blouse a perfect complement to her auburn hair. Glimmering gold jewelry adorns her neck and arms, stylish leather sandals on her dainty, suntanned feet. Green eyes highlighted with mascara. No rings.

"You look wonderful."

Madeline smiles and kisses my cheek.

"Single life has certain advantages," she says. "Not many, but some. After lying around the house for six weeks playing the jilted homemaker, I got mad, lost fifteen pounds, and took up tennis. I sent Cyril the bill for the lessons. Poor man. But enough of that. Let's sit out here and enjoy what's left of the sunset."

Madeline leads me out to the edge of the redwood stained deck to where three black wrought-iron rocking chairs sit facing west. Here and there along the shaded borders of the lawn are raised beds of impatiens and fledgling white caladiums. A cement birdbath stands upon a grassy knoll. Atop the horizon squats a huge orange fireball. I am still holding my briefcase.

"Let me have that," Madeline says.

She stands, takes the briefcase from me and stashes it behind her chair. She sits back down. I sit back down. We are now seated. Let the games begin.

"Speaking of Cyril," I say, "I had lunch with him yesterday. He seemed a little down in the dumps."

"He wants his cake and eat it, too," she says.

"His cake?"

Madeline laughs and brushes her auburn hair off her neck.

"He wants me, the kids, our old life together, provided he can keep his own apartment, his freedom to come and go as he pleases."

"His cake and eat it, too. And how about you, Madeline? What is it you want?"

Madeline turns to me, her green eyes narrowing.

"My life, such as it is," she says. "It's not what I expected, certainly not what I ever intended, but it's going to be all right."

Here she pauses, taking care to sweep some nonexistent lint off one leg of her satin slacks. The black fabric fits snugly about her thighs and hips. At her wrist a wide gold chain flashes in the orange sunlight.

"I've become more confident," she says. "Cyril and I were so young when we married, and he was so strong-willed, so determined to get where he wanted, that I just let him pull me right along. My entire life stood in the shadow of his."

"Do you miss it? Your old life?"

God! Skip the pleasantries about life with Cyril.

"Yes and no," she says. "I miss the part when the kids were young and we were just starting out. Cyril being hired by the university, moving here to Baton Rouge. Meeting so many new and different people. It was exciting. I don't miss what happened later. Our marriage failing. Cyril's ongoing trysts with his students. Do you have any idea what happens to men's minds when they start chasing twenty-year-old girls?"

They turn to salivating dogs. The question is, what do they talk about *after* sex?

"Are you ready for that drink?" Madeline asks, getting to her feet. "I won't be a minute. It's nice of you to stop by."

AFTER MADELINE LEAVES me to fetch the drinks, I manage the first decent breath of air since arriving on the topless patio. My diaphragm is knotted into a fist somewhere behind my breastbone.

It's nice of you to stop by, she said.

Well, not exactly. More like I slunk in through the back gate. Slipped the drunken sentry a few quid and have now managed to gain private audience with the queen. So now what? How to switch the agenda from finances to monkey business without seeming too crass? Keep the conversation spry and suggestive, yet friendly. After all, I suspect I'm not the first person to make an appearance on this patio in search of small favors. Nor am I the first man to ever make a trial run at a recently separated woman. It happens all the time. Were Sarah and I to part company, I could expect the same harsh treatment. Packs of horny men emerging from their dark dens with hopes of bedding my wife. Friends and neighbors nodding and sympathizing with my plight, pumping my hand, slapping me on the back, then trying to put it to my wife. It is a vile, contemptuous business, sex. Ruddy creatures with foul minds and swollen organs crawling over my wife's cake-scented flesh.

Goddamn.

Not that Sarah could ever be portrayed as vincible, some hapless southern belle at the mercy of a pack of shameless, marauding beasts. She is far too headstrong and proud and clever for that. Besides, Sarah likes a hand in the action as much as anyone. Nor is she above the clamor of the chase. It was Sarah, after watching me fumble around for days after our first meeting as college seniors, who finally took matters into her own hands and arranged that we go out together. Which, happily, led to bigger and better things. Until lately.

Sex: It's God's favorite practical joke on middle-aged men.

"That's all you think about anymore," Sarah said, just before turning out her bedside light last night.

"What do you mean?"

"The two things you think about — sex and death. That's *all* you think about."

"That's not true."

"Yes, it is," she said. "You're either worrying about dying or you're thinking about your little ding-ding."

"My little ding-ding?"

"It's all you ever think about."

"Little!"

"If you're so horny," she said, "why don't you do something about it for God's sake? Go out and get laid. Get a lover. Do something."

She reached over and hit the light switch, plunging the room into darkness.

"Just remember this, Gatlin, don't start something you don't want me to finish."

"HERE YOU ARE, kind sir," says Madeline, reappearing on the deck. "One ice-cold gin gimlet. Guaranteed to change your attitude if not your entire point of view."

Unless I am mistaken there has been a slight alteration in her appearance — telltale signs of a recent hair brushing, a touch of lip gloss, the faintest hint of cologne. Her tanned skin could use a proper licking.

"To getting on with one's life," I say, lifting my gimlet.

"And burying the dead," she says.

The normally harsh, metallic tang of the gin in my cocktail is offset by sweetened lime juice — high-powered jet fuel laced with sugar water. The upshot is a cold, clear, lubricious potion that numbs the lips and brain on contact. A certified icebreaker.

"So tell me, Madeline, are you seeing anyone in particular?"

"Oh, I go out, Gatlin. It's just most of the single men my age are divorced and hot on the trail of some twenty-two-year-old with three ounces of body fat who still thinks all men are like her daddy."

"There must be some, uh . . . normal men attracted to you?"

A normal man, with a kind heart and a gentle touch and a boundless sense of lust. Normal, like me.

"I never said men aren't attracted," she says, pointing one nut-brown foot toward the horizon. "Most of the *married* men I know are falling all over themselves. I've been grabbed, held, felt and mangled. I've got half the men in this neighborhood lining up for yard work, free oil changes, you name it. One of them gave me a set of steel wrenches."

"I'll bet you've become a hit with all the wives?"

Madeline falls back in her rocker and laughs.

"The wives! They're either terrified of me or they're

dying to trade places. They corner me at barbecues and cocktail parties and confess their marital woes, their infidelities. They're all curious about the quality of my life now that I've split with my husband of twenty years."

"What do you tell them?"

"I tell them to go home and try to work it out. That everything has its price."

Madeline takes a generous slug of her drink.

"So tell me, Gatlin," she says, turning in her seat. "Do all your clients merit these evening consultations? Or am I being granted the select treatment?"

"Well," I say, swigging my own gimlet. "Occasionally my clients have special needs."

"Special needs, how sweet," she says. "And your wife, Sarah? She's well?"

"Sarah's fine."

Two plump mourning doves come winging in low over the lawn and settle on the cement birdbath. Unaware of us, the birds step gingerly on maroon stick feet around the edge of the bath, taking cautious drinks. One movement from either of us will send them on their way.

"How long have you been married?" Madeline asks.

"Me? Twenty-four years," I say, watching the smeared images of two mourning doves disappear over the back fence into the failing light. "Twenty-five as of the end of next month."

"Let me hazard a guess," she says, a half-smile breaking out. "I'll just bet things between you and your wife aren't as fine as you pretend. I'm not saying you don't love each other, that you won't spend the rest of your lives together. But tell me, honestly, haven't things grown just a little stale? Just the tiniest little bit?"

The hunter becomes the hunted.

"Well now, Madeline, *stale*, that's an offensive word."

"Let me tell you what I would like," she says, rattling the ice in her empty glass so violently that several of the cubes clatter to the deck floor. "I would like another drink. You interested?"

"Well, if it's not too much. . . . That is, as long as you are having . . . ," I say, staring down into my own glass that I have suddenly begun shaking like a maraca. "I mean, yes, another drink would be perfect."

Without another word, she takes my glass and proceeds up the wooden deck to the side door off the kitchen.

"Madeline, I hope you don't think. . . . That you won't construe. . . . I guess my coming here is a bit of a surprise?"

Smiling, Madeline brushes a strand of auburn hair behind one ear.

"No," she says. "It is not."

Part V

Friday, June 8

Before Sunrise

Chapter 13

FOR YEARS my father claimed he could float on his back in the bathtub. He told my sister and me that he could float on the morning dew. He told us floating was like baldness or blue eyes, and either you had it or you did not. My mother, even after much practice in a neighbor's pool, sank straight to the bottom like a stone the instant she quit swimming. The art of floating eludes her to this day.

What the physical act of floating on water meant to my father, what thoughts, sensations came to him as he drifted there in our neighbor's pool are obscure riddles upon which I might forever ruminate. I have, nonetheless, made inference — the small relief he must have felt by rising atop his seething anxieties; his feeling of pride in the execution of a simple feat unequaled by his wife or his two young children; his sense of joy in the graceful denial of gravity and the uncommon weight of human dread.

And yet there was more. As he floated there on the pool's unrippled surface, his eyes shut tight, a slight, enigmatic smile upon his lips, there was a certain radiance about him. He had the face of a sleeping child.

Chapter 14

In THE LONG MONTHS of summer here beside the river in Baton Rouge, it's the heat — steamy, stifling, omnipresent and unforgiving. I did not mention inconvenient. Every summer the front door of my house swells in the high humidity and will not close or open, relegating all comings and goings to the back door off the muggy garage. My hair gets frizzy and limp, the sheetrock walls of the bedroom sweat, my backyard becomes a vine-choked, sweltering Congo. A peculiar pink mold thrives in the toilet bowl.

And the heat is unrelenting. My entire person is bathed in a perpetual salty sheen. My feet are hot and my socks are wet — my underwear is permanently crack-bound. The scuttling hordes of giant tree roaches inhabiting the kitchen are pursuing cooler quarters. The cat naps all day long with its tongue stuck out; my car runs poorly and the birds stop singing. Even the hateful yellow jackets take to the deep shade. I seek dry, conditioned air. I lie shirtless under the whirling ceiling fan, wildly dreaming or bolt awake, reckoning the days till mid-October and the first blessed cool front.

Four months and counting.

It's almost 5:00 A.M. and I have been lying here in the dark for an hour trying to guess which panting breath will be my last. My bucking heart insists on throwing itself against the blue wall of my chest, jumping first here, then lunging there, as if it were trying to free itself from my body, scamper off down the hall into some remote corner and hide. It sputters, pops, leaps to one side like the cartoon version of an old automobile engine and then fires. My breath wheezes.

Jesus.

LAST NIGHT'S telephone calls began early and lasted until late.

"If that phone rings one more time, I'm going to pitch it in the trash."

"That'll show them," Sarah said, rising from the kitchen table. "Give it to that nice trashman like you did our television. Poor man could probably use a telephone."

Sarah retrieved the portable phone from the countertop and set it beside my plate of warmed-over spaghetti.

"Make up your mind," she said. "I'm going to take my shower."

By the tenth ring I lost my resolve and answered the thing.

"Hello?"

"It's me," Rusty said over a din of loud music and background noise.

He was calling from some bar — not a promising sign. Though he would deny it, Rusty's affable nature fades after a few cocktails.

"Apologize," he said.

Two presumptions spring to mind: Either my old friend has learned that I did stumble across the budding romance between Julie and Cyril Newman and, unlike a true friend, failed to inform him that his wife may be sleeping with another man. Or he's pissed because I made light of his being in love with Madame X.

"Apologize for what?"

"If you knew her, you would understand," Rusty said.

"What makes you think I don't know her?"

"Trust me," he said, "you don't know her. She's like pure sunlight, like walking around in a bolt of yellow sunlight. She's warm and tender and alive. She's insatiable and curious and happy. She's unlike any woman I've ever known."

"If I were you, Rusty, I wouldn't underrate Julie's ability to decode your behavior. She's not stupid."

"You're recommending I straighten up and fly right?"

There followed a long pause during which I figured Rusty had either passed out or was now on his way over to punch me in the mouth.

"If I could find someone to do the job right," he said, finally, "I'd pay the son-of-a-bitch to fuck her. I'm serious. It might do Julie some good. As long as they could do the deed without making a big fuss out of it, I'd be happy for them. I'd pay the bastard myself."

"You're in a world of trouble, my friend."

"I'm not giving her up, goddamnit!" Rusty said. "You hear me? And neither would you."

I NO SOONER CONCLUDED my conversation with Rusty than the phone rang again. Perhaps life without a telephone wasn't such a bad idea.

"Hey, it's me," Matt said. "I just checked Saturday morning's weather forecast — sunny, clear and warm. Perfect day for river travel."

"That's great, Matt. You bet. I cleared everything with Sarah so Saturday morning is definitely on. You've got the canoe all lined up?"

"Funny you should ask," he said. "Matter of fact, I could use some help. We need a car to get the canoe down to the river."

"I think I can handle that. What else?"

"Something to eat?"

"I'll take care of the food and drinks."

"Fantastic!" he said. "You're going to love it out there, man. Once you put the mean city behind you, you're going to love it. It's like no place you've ever been."

"O.K., Matt, we've got the canoe, food and drinks. What else?"

"That ought to cover it," he said. "I'll bring a jug of water and the tobacco."

"Tobacco?"

"For trade with the Indians."

"The Indians, right. I keep forgetting about those Indian

spirits of yours. O.K., sounds like we're definitely in business. Anything else?"

All I heard was Matt's quiet breathing on the other end of the line.

"I talked with my mom tonight," he said at last. "Everything's cool, pretty much. She's still dealing with my moving out of the house. I know she wanted to ask all kinds of questions but she held herself back. She didn't even cry."

"Talk to Rick?"

"He was out," Matt said. "If he wants to lend a helping hand to every whacked-out hobo in Baton Rouge, that's his business. You're either with him or against him."

"Just give a listen to what he has to say and don't take it personally."

"Don't take it personally?" he said. "It's like living with the frigging Pope or something. Every second, every minute of your whole life has got to revolve around some grand purpose or it's not worth anything. It's all or nothing with him. It's not any fun. No fun. You hear what I'm saying? There's no time for just hanging out, having fun. Much less something as pointless as a canoe trip down the river. You hear me?"

I heard him. I've had similar thoughts myself, more than once. It was a fine line.

"I want you to know it's more complicated than that, Matt. People do things — all of us — we do and say things and it affects everyone around us in ways no one could have figured. We struggle, we do the best we can, but none of us is perfect. Rick's not perfect either. Just take him for what he is and go on about your business."

"It's *my* life," he said. "It's mine. He has no right to tell me what to believe or how to live."

ONE SUMMER night seven years ago, Rick, king of the midnight ramblers, piled into his car for the short drive from my house over to his place. It was only six blocks. Four stop signs and one traffic light. Who could have figured? What is the likelihood of one six-minute drive altering the context of a person's life? Rick sailed down the moonlit side street toward the green traffic light at Stanford Avenue and into the intersection where he broadsided the small speeding vehicle. The driver of the small car, himself in a near-drugged stupefaction, was unharmed. His teenage girlfriend, however, was thrown from the car fullface into a utility pole, shattering her skull, neck and pelvis and both legs. She died twice on the short drive to the hospital only to be revived by emergency medical personnel. She spent four months in a frightening halo neck-brace and a year and a half in painful rehabilitation. Plastic surgeons rebuilt her jaw and the right side of her face. Most of her memory eventually returned. Rick and the other driver were both handcuffed, booked and jailed. The desk sergeant phoned Rick's wife.

Even when sober, Rick refused any attempt at bail and all manner of lawful or constructive counsel by friends and family. When I visited him, he wouldn't make eye contact. Two days later, the man who walked free into the bright sunlight had an odd look in his eye. The full scope of the accident, coupled with his own witless involvement, seemed to have penetrated not only Rick's psyche but the makeup of his bones and blood cells as well, slightly altering what was there. Outwardly he still appeared to be the same person, tall and lanky with a loping giddy-up stride, still possessing the aggravating knack for telling others what *he thought* was in their own best interest, but he was changed. He stopped chasing the moon and stars across the sky on Friday and Saturday nights. He started teaching literacy classes at the parish prison on weekends. Eventually he quit his newspaper job and took over a drug outreach program funded by the city.

As might be expected, Rick's sober transformation took its toll on relations with a few of his old friends. Not only had the group lost its best incendiary, but here was one of our number suddenly possessed of an agenda that did not concur with our own. A few of us misread his change in behavior as a rebuke of our characters. Meanwhile, even Rick's attendance at the obligatory barbecues became the genesis of mild comedy, usually at his expense.

So, tell me, Rick, do you take lime or a lemon with your tap water?

Chapter 15

STILL IN MY BED in the humid dark. The glowing red digits on the clock face now read 5:16 A.M. The clock has a variety of alarm options should I be required to awake at a specified time. Should I ever fear oversleeping.

An article in yesterday's paper reported that suicide rates for Americans age sixty-five or older have jumped twenty-one percent in recent years. Divorced and widowed white males are experiencing the highest rates. All over this land trembling fingers are lifting guns, prescription bottles, spoons of poison to venerable lips and temples and snuffing out the life within. Think of it. After all those years of working, raising families, paying taxes, buying down mortgages, death suddenly becoming preferable to life. Darkness to light.

Friendships live and die, too. And no one is left unscathed by these shifting alliances. With the notable exceptions of Rusty and Rick, relations between my extended family of old college friends have been deteriorating for years. It is a disturbing, complicated business. At bottom I think we simply took the nature of our community for granted. That we failed to realize an old friend gets priority. Some of us made so much money that we outstripped the others' ability to join in on the fun. How can someone be expected to partake of the convivial champagne toast if he cannot afford the bill of fare? So many embittered riffraff milling at the front gate.

But the dissolution of the tribe entailed more than a discrepancy of money, more than who got to feast on the most tea and sugar cakes. It had more to do with failed kindnesses and violated trusts — with misjudged overtures and bungled affections and inadvertent, senseless remarks taken out-of-context.

The collapse of our family was mostly about change, people growing older and less compliant. And the reluctance of old friends to sanction the result.

The demise of old friendships is almost unbearable. Like losing an arm or a leg to some dreaded cancer. You are going to beat it, you are unblinking in your absolute will to survive, but inwardly you mourn.

IT'S A WONDER I ever sleep. Lying here in the dark with a rage of memories running through my brain half the night, every night. Heart-stricken, past-possessed, lusting, miserable son-of-a-bitch! Give it a rest.

Not all of Sarah's several pregnancies ended in wayward miscarriage. One of them, the harrowing finale, ran days short of full term only to have the child tangle himself in the umbilical cord and suffocate in the womb, leaving us spent and without comment or solace in the presence of a perfectly formed blue baby. I remember Sarah waking me from a deep sleep and describing the lifeless weight in her abdomen.

"He's not moving," she said softly. "He hasn't moved once all night. He's not going to move."

Sarah seemed oddly possessed of herself, unshaken by the rude, inopportune stillness, almost contemplative. She might have been rendering a dream or a memory from the distant past.

"It so unfair," she said absently. "All I want is a child to love, a part of you and me to care for. Why is that so difficult? Why are we having to suffer this?"

After being roused from her own sleep, Sarah's doctor told us not to worry, that a period of relative immobility in late pregnancy was no reason to panic.

"Calm down," she said, "I'll meet you at the hospital in half an hour."

Doctor Cole was an attractive woman in her late thirties, sported a deep bronze suntan and short haircut, and seemed so distracted you might think she disliked her work. The nurse and I stayed flattened against the examining room wall to give her space. The tanned physician shuffled, spun, muttering her medical lingo in a flat, distracted voice that was hypnotizing. I couldn't help perceiving the gory, far-flung trail of limbs and tissues, fetuses, organs and bones, stretching out behind her like some fantastic new zodiac. A teeming night sky of human remnants.

In the midst of every bad fucking thing that's ever happened to me, in the moment of its origin, I've always felt partly responsible, that somehow I had it coming, that if I paid more attention, lived better, worked harder, it would not have gone so badly. That anything I might have done would have been better than what I did.

What came next was a kind of personalized hell, tailored to meet our worst nightmares. After eleven hours of drug-induced labor, after a painful ordeal of deep breathing, teeth gnashing, alternate blowing, cramping, weeping, bellowing, crying out to heaven, and pushing, pushing, pushing, Sarah gave birth to a sleeping blue baby.

"He should be mourned," Sarah said, big tears racing down her cheeks.

The misery of that moment is undiminished by time.

"His passing should be grieved," Sarah cried. "Do something!"

"Hold on, easy now," I said, taking both her clenched fists in my hands and kissing them. "Slow down. Everything is going to be all right here. We still have each other. We'll always have each other. No matter what."

"Promise?"

"I promise."

NOW THAT EVERY drunk in town has possession of my home phone number, I can anticipate irate calls on an hourly basis. Cliff phoned, too, late last night, full of grit and vigor as usual.

"Hey, son, you still among the living?" he said. "I figured you'd be abed with Ma in her see-through kerchief. Come have a drink with me!"

"In your next life, Cliff, you're returning as a mongrel dog."

"Does that mean I'm having fun?" he said. "What's a pitiful old man do for fun? Is it still legal at your age? Having fun, I mean."

"Well, for starters, I'm going on a canoe ride down the Mississippi."

"The river? Hold on, I think we got a bad connection here."

Cliff rapped his receiver several times against a hard surface.

"Hello?" he said, getting back on the line. "Did you say Mississippi? As in the river? In a canoe? Are you drunk?"

"I'm not drunk, Cliff. I'm meeting a friend Saturday morning with a canoe and we're going to put it in the Mississippi. Paddle right down the spanking middle of it. You want to come along?"

"You forget, son," he scoffed. "I'm from Vicksburg. I've heard enough gruesome stories about the Mississippi to last me a lifetime. Alligators, wild dogs, panthers, quicksand, undertows, river hooligans. . . . Only a damn fool would go out there looking for trouble."

"We're going Saturday morning, Cliff, panthers or no panthers."

"Suit yourself, old timer. I'll stay behind and mingle with the women folk, keep their lonesome spirits up. I'm a younger man with nothing to prove. Say, you ever took a rocket ride?"

"What?"

"The closer she gets to orgasm," he said, "the more the whites of her eyes begin to show."

"Jesus."

"It's my job just to keep up a steady rhythm, don't talk,

let her concentrate. When her mouth drops open and her eyes roll all the way back in her head —"

"I get the picture, Cliff."

"With both her eyes wide open and just the whites showing, it's like fucking a voodoo queen."

"I'm glad we had this little chat, Cliff. It's always a pleasure. So, tell me, anything new and interesting in your life? Talked to your children lately?"

Cliff's normally crisp rejoinder failed to materialize.

"I'm no longer a proud papa," he said simply. "I am now the good Uncle Wiggly. Woeful, old Uncle Wiggly, holed up in his faraway house, living off his woman flesh and sumptuous drink. Papa is gone now, long live Uncle Wiggly. Come have a drink with me."

"Can't do it."

"So, how's about you, son?" Cliff said, rattling the ice in his glass. "Is there fire in the big boiler? Does the choo choo still enter the station?"

"As we grow older, Cliff, wiser, we learn that sex is only a minor figment in the grand scheme of things. Like the notion of a good night's sleep, the idea of ever getting filthy rich, sex is something we leave behind."

"Sounds like you're not getting any."

Chapter 16

SEATED ALONE at the edge of the topless patio last night, I waited for Madeline to return with the second round of sugary gimlets. As the twilight descended, I worked myself into a full-blown frenzy. Nursed by the cold gin and the gathering dark, my heightened imagination led me to believe that I was being watched, that somewhere in the surrounding azalea beds lay Madeline's distraught husband Cyril. Was he a man, I wondered, easily induced to violence? I could almost sense his wild dismay. Hiding like an animal in the dense, insect-laden shrubbery of his former home, the sickening incredulity of watching his own wife having truck with another man. *My* bare paws caressing the scented flesh. A wanton look of craving in his spouse's eye.

"You look like a man who could use a stiff drink," Madeline said, appearing with the gimlets.

In the azalea beds, not a creature was stirring.

"What I want and what I normally get don't always coincide," I said.

"Here's to everyone getting more of what he can use," she said, tapping her glass against the side of mine.

Madeline and I splashed around in our gin drinks for a moment, allowing the jet fuel to work its clear magic. From the dense shrubbery rose the shrill melody of summer insects.

Get on with it.

"I was hoping it might work out like this, Madeline. I mean just the two of us . . . drinks. Conversation. I mean you and I hardly know each other. Anything could happen. It's as if we've been given this private time of our own here. Just the two of us."

Madeline glared at me over the top of her gimlet drink.

"You know, Madeline, it's what we don't know that sometimes interests us the most. The two of us here together, away from everything. No one else knowing what happens. What we say, what we do. That's part of the beauty of it. Being alone with another person, someone new. Getting inside another person's skin. And it being a secret. That's the best part. Getting close and no one knowing."

Madeline turned slightly in her wrought-iron chair, recrossed her shapely legs, then sipped from her drink. Now that I had framed my cryptic overture, would she take it? Why wouldn't she take it?

"I've had about as much sex with unhappy men as I can stand," she said, shaking her head. "I'm not a prude, you know. Since Cyril and I split up, I've been *close,* as you put it, with several men."

"Several?"

"More than two. Less than six," she said, frowning. "Don't worry, it's no one you would possibly know."

"I know lots of people in this town, Madeline."

"Trust me," she said, "you don't know them. But do you know what I did enjoy? More than all the goofy attention, all the fumbling in the dark? Can you guess?"

The endless tide of whooping orgasms.

"It was the laughter," she said. "I had forgotten the pure pleasure of being made to laugh."

"Cyril didn't make you laugh?"

"He did once. He was once the funniest man I ever met. But then he changed. Now he saves his humor for his students. That and his vast love of sex."

Madeline raises her glass in mock tribute.

"Hail Cyril and his mighty club!"

"His club?"

Madeline sighed and stared off into the growing blackness overhead.

"Cyril has an enormous penis," she said. "Sometimes it could be unpleasant. At least it was for me."

"His penis."

Swell. Good-looking and single and with a big dick. No wonder Julie looked as if she had just won the lottery.

"Oh, I'm sure it's an asset with today's youth," Madeline said. "The dapper professor and his throbbing scepter."

Madeline dipped once more into her gimlet and shut her green eyes. If she were holding a big enough grudge against Cyril, my timing might be perfect. She opened her eyes, then spoke.

"You're a nice man," she said, "and I appreciate your

listening to me babble on like this, but you do realize that I'm not going to have sex with you?"

And just like that I was out of the saddle, shot down, sitting on stupid.

"You've misunderstood me," I said feebly.

"I don't think so," Madeline said. "What you had in mind was a few laughs, a little hot sex, and no one gets attached, no one gets her feelings hurt, am I right? And then you beat it on home to your wife and I crawl in bed alone. Sorry, I'm through with that."

Had I misidentified the randy Madame *X*? Misread the signs and jumped to a conclusion?

Now it was my turn to twist in my seat, stretch my legs, drink, cast about for something to say. *The first time she says no*, Cliff said, *she means yes.*

"Are you still in love with Cyril?" I said.

I couldn't stop myself. I opened my mouth and the words flew right out.

"What an absurd question," she said, one hand flaying at the darkened sky above our heads. "Of course I love him! I despise him. I loathe the blood that flows through his filthy, stinking veins. There you have it. I love him and I hate him. More or less, depending upon the time of day and which way the wind is blowing."

Madeline set her drink down on the deck floor, put her hands together between her knees, and sighed.

"You want to hear a story?" she said after a minute. "It's not a pretty story."

"Tell me."

Please. Do, say anything. Get me off the hook here.

Madeline rattled the heavy gold chain on her wrist and took a deep breath. She spoke slowly, as if measuring each word.

"One day last fall I took Cyril's car to be cleaned and washed. In one corner of the trunk I found a videocassette. At first I didn't think anything about it, but something struck me as odd. When I got back home, I brought the video in with me and put it in the tape player. Instantly a man and a girl appeared on the television screen. The camera was aimed at the man's bare back so at first it was difficult to determine what was what. The girl was young, seventeen, eighteen, I'm not sure, but very pretty. She was holding her little tits in her hands for the man to suckle. *Do it, yes, please! Do it now!* she pleaded. I sat there watching him lick that child's breasts like a dog. Only when he spoke did I know for sure it was Cyril."

Madeline fell back in her rocker and clasped her hands atop her head. After a pause she retrieved her drink from the deck floor and took a small sip. She wiped her eyes on the backs of her hands and resumed her slow speech.

"Cyril abandoned the girl's tits and started nuzzling his way down her stomach toward her crotch. He mumbled sweet nothings as he went. *Oh, baby, baby, baby, you're so fine. So pretty and so fine. Oh, baby.* That's what he always says. *That's* what he always said to me. For twenty years I listened to those words! The very same words. *Oh, baby, baby, sweet baby, I'm going to eat you up.* I sat there watching the big white dog lick the girl's vagina."

A star-speckled sky had appeared over Baton Rouge and the topless patio. The ice cubes had melted in my nearly full gimlet. It no longer occurred to me that what the Lady Madeline needed was a really good screwing.

"But you know," she said, wiping mascara from under her eyes. "I wish I could say I've been through absolute hell but now it's better and I never look back. I wish I could say that."

I wished I had a deep hole I could crawl into.

Chapter 17

LEAVING Madeline's house and the deep, green lawns of Kenilworth subdivision behind, I had tried to assess just how big a wretch I had made of myself. Was it possible to be any more beastly or just plain rude? Where did my mind go sometimes? Could a man be insane and still out walking around, conducting business, living his life? If a person can still feel shame, is there need for reparation?

I eased down Perkins Road and turned left onto Essen Lane, which was lit up like daytime. A steady stream of nighttime traffic flowed in and out of the many offices, shops, banks, cafés and bars. Copeland's New Orleans Style Restaurant looked jammed. The parking lot outside India's Restaurant was overflowing. The Bamboo Garden had a line out the front door. Even the fast-food joints were jumping. The neon spectacle of urban America had arrived, and everyone was in a hurry to be there. Still reeling from the gimlet drinks, I reminded myself to keep an eye peeled for cops and speeding teenagers.

Home, unruly prince, home to long-legged wife and cozy bed-chamber.

THE PHONE was ringing when I walked in the back door. It was for Sarah. I found her in the bedroom studying a road map.

"The phone's for you, Sarah. It's Stephen."

She talked for no more than a minute, then hung up.

"Let me guess, Sarah. Stephen's having a little car trouble and needs a lift to t'ai chi?"

"You missed your calling," she said, "you should have been a detective.

"Very funny. What's wrong with his car?"

"He didn't elaborate. Would you like me to have him drop by so you could take a look at it?"

"There must be other people in the class, why does he always call you?"

"I think he's cute. He makes me laugh."

"He makes you laugh?" I said. "He's an eighteen-year-old kid who can't afford to fix his own car. The last time I saw him his socks didn't match."

AFTER CONSUMING last night's warmed-over garlic spaghetti supper, I slipped into the bathroom for a good mouth scrubbing. It's gotten to where even brushing my teeth has become a horror. Because my gums have steadily retreated away from the base of my teeth, it looks as if I've grown fangs. Under the fluorescent lights of the mirror, my coloring takes on motley undertones. My skin looks bleached out, dry and old. The frozen scowl on my face bespeaks a sentiment beyond the living.

ONE BY ONE my father's friends are dying. Assorted cancers, heart attacks, strokes, aneurysms, one accidental poisoning. Every six months or so my mother will phone me up out of the clear blue and inform me in a weary, resigned tone of voice the name of the latest departed. And while she seems vaguely annoyed by this slow attrition, I find it appalling. These men were icons, iron figures from my youth. They were the strongest, most vivid symbols of my gender. I literally sat at their feet and learned how to be a man. How to think and work and have fun, how to respond to children and the world around me, as well as a kind of dumb, self-serving regard for women. These men were products of their times. They smoked and drank too much, they worked too hard, they took for granted their rowdy good health and their strong wives and young families and their own blind luck. And now, after only a few decades and with few exceptions, those who have survived have grown old and diminished, so many lonesome bone-bags biding their precious time. I picture the group of them seated round the campfire in a fading light, trying to unravel the past. The future is near and it is certain.

Back home for the holidays last Christmas, I accompany my mother on a trip to the Veteran's Hospital to visit what's left of Duncan Emes, longtime friend of my father. For Duncan, these are troubled times. A victim of mouth and throat cancer, he speaks with the aid of a hand-held microphone which he places over what remains of his voice box. The gadget reduces his speech to an eerie, metallic droning and slows the pace of conversation to a crawl. What's happening inside his ruined mouth is too gruesome to describe.

But Duncan is in an exceptionally good mood upon our arrival and, in between fits of laughter and choking, reminisces about the old days. He tells my mother the story of his setting fire to the duck blind in the cold salt water marsh and nearly drowning trying to escape. He recalls the time I found him drunk and singing Christmas carols on his deer stand at sunset and led him safely back through the deep woods to camp — a young boy and his besotted Santa elf. He tells me once again that my father was the finest man with whom he ever hunted.

As Duncan lies there recounting his stories, giving fluid form to the unruly past, I am caught up by his telling of it. Seen from the present day, all the hunting and fishing trips with my father and his hard-driving companions take on a broader consequence. Those weekend excursions were the occasion for a circle of men to congregate in a place and manner of their own choosing and, for some of them at least, be altered by it. Or perhaps in spite of it. Because what strikes me most about those long ago weekends is not the hundreds of bitter cold mornings and endless winter afternoons I spent sitting alone on a stand or in a blind, listening, watching, waiting, trying to still my runaway mind, but rather the intense moments of fellowship, the story-telling and rustic cooking and camaraderie shared between good friends around a wood fire.

When it's time to conclude our hospital visit, I take Duncan's wasted hand in both of mine and tell him how good it is to see him again. I tell him on my next visit home the two of us will make a drive out to the hunting camp, just like in the old days. Duncan agrees, sounding out his metallic enthusiasm, but I see death smiling in his eyes.

It's impossible to think of Duncan Emes without thinking of my father, the two men who watched over my childhood. The two men who shaped my thinking.

One hot September night when I am sixteen — mother is away at a book convention in Dallas — my father bursts into my bedroom. The wild look is on him.

"Talk to me," he says. "Talk. Do something. Just keep talking."

"It's the middle of the night," I moan, pulling the cover over my head. "School starts tomorrow."

"Talk to me," he says, closing the bedroom door. "If you don't talk to me this instant, I'll die."

Standing there barefoot in his underwear in the half-light, the perspiration running down his face and arms and onto the floor at his feet, his two hands pawing at the air in front of him, I think if I do not say the right things, right then, right there, he might die.

"If you don't talk," he says, "I'll die."

I sit up so fast I almost roll out of the bed. And then I start to talk, saying anything, nonsense, speaking as fast as the words will come. I tell him about my two close friends at school, I describe their looks, their characters, both good and bad. I reminisce about the family's trip to the Ozark Mountains a couple of years earlier to see the leaves change. I talk about the many hunting trips the two of us had made together, about his lunatic hunting partner, Duncan Emes. I tell the stories of the burning duck blind and the besotted Santa elf. I make up things as I go. My father just stands there with his back against the door, his teeth chattering, staring at the floor. After about an hour, I run out of gas.

"Don't stop," he says. "I'm afraid."

I am sixteen years old; my father's mind is coming unraveled there in front of me and I have to do something, so I suggest we go for a walk.

"Just don't stop talking."

I put on jeans and a shirt, fetch my father's shoes and outlandish purple bathrobe, and we ease out the front door, locking my sister in behind us. In the deserted street, we begin to walk.

"Talk to me," he says.

I tell him some of my earliest memories are of Duncan Emes standing over the campstove, a cigarette dangling from his lips, cooking. It might be catfish or snipe or venison or ducks or geese or squirrels or quail or doves, it never really mattered. Often as not, he cooked enough food for a banquet just on the off chance enough people would show up to eat it, if for no other reason, than it provided a trapped audience to whom he could present his one-man comedy show. Everything Duncan did, he did in a big rowdy way. A glass of lip-smacking cold beer, a bowl of ice cream, a cigarette, a loud rousing fart. He seemed to enjoy life for its own sake.

My father never says a word. He walks slowly by my side, eyes on the ground, listening, nodding his head, but never speaks.

I describe, probably exaggerated, my worst childhood

fears. I boast of my wildest ambitions. I tell him what I want to do, where I want to go, what I want to be like when I grow up. I am a child unburdening himself to a parent.

We walk by the library, on past the high school, out beyond the last of the new subdivisions, out to the edge of the city limits. In the open fields we watch the first light glisten in the wet grasses. Snatches of ground fog tumble end over end. The birds wake. With the rising sun, my father's terror seems to leave him.

"You must be exhausted," he says.

Back at our house, father helps me off with my shoes and socks and steers me back to bed. Before I drop off, he tells me that I can sleep late and miss the first day of school. He tells me not to worry.

"You are a strong person," he says. "Always remember that. And you and your sister are a blessing to your mother and me. And wherever you go, whatever you do, we'll be there with you. Now go to sleep."

That's what he says.

Maybe I should know what's going to happen next. Maybe if I were older, a little smarter, I could tell more Duncan stories and keep my father's mind from crossing over to the other side. I might charge in like the daring hero I've always wanted to be and stop him. But I am only sixteen years old and out of gas, and I fall asleep.

With both his children asleep inside the house, my father starts his car and attaches one end of the vacuum cleaner hose to the tailpipe, intending to run the opposite end through the backseat window. Only the vacuum hose doesn't reach the rear window. It lacks about a foot. He abandons the vacuum hose, shucks his purple bathrobe and lies face up on the wet grass under the chugging exhaust pipe, gulping the fumes. It takes many breaths, I've always imagined, many deep and committed breaths before he slips into unconsciousness.

It is still early that morning when my sister awakes, wondering where everybody is on the first day of school. In the backyard she discovers the automobile's engine still running, the body beneath.

Chapter 18

IT IS NOW 5:42 A.M. and the world outside my bedroom window has grown still and seemingly absent of all sentient life, and yet I cannot shut my burning, bloodshot eyes.

To sleep, perchance to dream. . . .

It is only after I grew older, more seasoned, that I was able to contemplate my father's suicide without being overrun by the emotions of anguish and guilt. I had graduated from L.S.U. and married before I could even speak of his death without the attendant sensations of nausea and vertigo toward the manner of his demise, its desperate craving.

But as time passed and I moved deeper into and finally out of the narrow, self-distorting tunnel of young adulthood, I began to slowly sort out my emotions. And, if little else, the broad vista of middle age offers a vantage point from which to view past and future with equal light and weight. As of Wednesday, I am forty-seven, the age of my father at the time of his death. This hardly seems possible — not his dying, not only that, but that the two of us have finally attained, if only in regard to the passage of time, a kind of level footing, a fleeting parity. And that there he is to remain forever, fixed in my memory, while I must venture onward.

In one of my favorite daydreams I picture him floating on his back in the middle of a great blue ocean, his feet crossed, his arms outstretched, shooting a stream of cool water out of his mouth and back over his shoulder. He smiles and wiggles all ten of his toes. In the wide sky above him there is not a single bird or wisp of cloud. Despite the surge of the ocean's current, the action of the wind, my father drifts steadily onward, unhurried and unperturbed.

The envy of every floater.

SLEEP, the blue-hulled vessel running somewhere off the coast of my consciousness, eludes me. At least my heart has ceased trying to leap out of its socket. Praise Allah. Not knowing if the next lunging thud of my heart pump will burst its seams and send me hurtling naked and unprepared into who-knows-what. I'm too young to die! I've got my whole life. . . .

Calm down. Fluff up the pillow there, old boy. Take a deep breath.

Relax.

Perhaps I could take up meditation? I read somewhere rhythmic chanting is advised for soothing the harried nervous system. Imagine. Me in my flowing chiffon robes sitting here through the long night chanting some ancient religious text. Incense and candles burning in all four corners of the room, prayer wheels spinning and brass bells ringing. At peace and enlightened and commingling with the stratosphere. Mantras chiming like sacred music off the vaulted ceiling of my skull. My overwrought nerve endings growing as limp and pliable as cooked pasta.

Sarah would have a fit, move herself and all her possessions lock, stock and barrel into the refurbished guest room. And once she's barricaded in there, I can kiss what's left of our sexual congress a sweet goodbye.

On second thought, no chanting.

Masturbation? I'm too old. Prayer? But to whom? I know full well what some people would say to that: Just pray and don't worry about the who on the other end of the line. Prayer, I've heard it said, is its own end. Prayer is God communing with Himself. This latter notion strikes me as particularly fantastic. Old Father God and I, two late night Titans, wide awake and crooning through the long dark, whispering bits of glad tidings and swapping jokes. Solemn amendments and the willing quid pro quo.

I just don't get it.

Then again, it occurs to me a prudent man might hedge his bets and pray anyway. Seek out instruction and hope to maintain damage control.

Dear Lord of Hosts and Creator of the Singing Spheres, I am a worthless, helplessly self-centered, pitiful, lusting clown but long to do better. Send help.

These days, of course, everyone is free to advance his own ideas about God, where He would best fit into the overall picture, how She might best serve our individual needs. God, like music or clothing, has become but one more festooned commodity in a crowded street bazaar where we take what we want from wherever we can find it so long as it makes us feel good about ourselves.

I AWOKE on my forty-seventh birthday to a cup of black coffee and the sight of a starving, emaciated child with flies swarming on his face and runny eyes. It sickened me. One of the morning news channels, in an effort to capture the outrage of the child's plight, had broadcast his portrait live and uncensored into the pale light of my living room. The boy's mother, herself a wasted bag-a-bones, sat nearby rocking on her haunches and keening a tearless lament. Behind her flickered images of half-starved men and women, children, hacking at the dry earth. They appeared to be digging either a water well or shallow grave. It was of no comfort to me to realize that by the time I could do anything, write a check, call my representative, this child's suffering would have ceased. All of this in living vivid color, no less.

I lugged my television out to the trash cans by the street.

I OUGHT to have my head examined. Donate my libido to science. First things first, I'll write Madeline a note today thanking her for the gin gimlets and wishing her the best with her own travails. I might address a few minor changes in her retirement accounts, try to pass on a few investment tips she can use. All things said and done, she let me down rather gracefully.

"Madeline," I said, the two of us walking casually down

her driveway to my car, "I believe I owe you an apology. After all you went through, *are* going through, I feel like a creep."

"Don't worry about me," she said, touching my arm. "You're just confused. Acting on some bad advice, maybe. Take my advice and go home and make love to your wife."

IN BED BESIDE ME, Sarah lifts one bare leg from beneath the sheet and throws it over my hip. She moans in her sleep.

"Sarah. Sarah, wake up. You're dreaming."

"Hhmmm?"

"Sarah, wake up."

"What?"

"You're dreaming."

Sarah sits bolt upright in the bed and looks at me, then collapses back onto the pillow.

"Damn."

"Are you all right?"

"It's hot in here," she says, kicking the sheet onto the floor.

"Tell me about it."

"What?"

"Your dream. Tell me about it."

Sarah blinks, then covers her face with her hands. After a moment she removes her hands and opens her eyes. She looks intently at the ceiling as if her dream is showing there.

"I'm standing before a mirror in the corner of a room.

An old-fashioned room ... with high ceilings and tall windows. I'm wearing a long silk gown, a black ribbon round my neck. Velvet slippers on my feet. But something is missing. Then a shape ... a figure appears in the mirror behind me. It's a man — he's dressed in some kind of uniform, military I think — but I can't see his face.

" *'Try this'*, he says, placing a hat on my head.

"It's a big, summer hat with a wide brim that hangs down over my eyes. All I can see are my feet and his feet. His hands. He puts his hands on my hips.

" *'Do not be afraid'*, he says.

"Slowly, he slides his hands up from my hips, across my stomach, stopping just below my breasts. I can feel the warmth from his hands through my gown.

" *'Do not be afraid'*, he says.

"Someone will see us, I tell him, trying to look out from under the brim of the hat. My heart is racing.

" *'No one will see us'*, he says.

"They'll walk in and see us together, I tell him. I can feel his breath on the back of my neck, his body nestling against mine. His hands are moving. . . ."

"So what happened then, Sarah?"

"That's when you woke me up."

"Anyone we know?" I ask.

"Who?"

"Prince Charming in the mirror glass."

"I couldn't see his face."

"Ah, well, that's comforting. Some mystery man in a uniform is running his hands all over you. Is there anything we need to talk about?"

Sarah rolls over against my side and yawns. I slip my arm around her shoulder.

"It was just a dream," she says.

JUNE 8TH. Day one hundred sixty of this year's sojourn round the yellow sun. Moon phase: full. Thirteen days till the official start of summer. Forecast: partly cloudy, hot and humid. Twenty percent chance of rain. Heat Index approaching 100 degrees. No relief in sight.

In the darkness before sunrise, a moment's tender peace.

Sarah dozes with her head on my shoulder, her breathing slow and rhythmic. Her skin smells like cake.

"Sarah."

"Hmmm?"

"I think we should go out west together."

Her blue eyes snap bright as candles.

"Out west," I say. "Over the rainbow. Wherever it is you want to go this summer, we should go together. I think it's important we go together."

In the dim light, Sarah eyes search every crease and wrinkle of my face. She grabs me with both hands.

"You mean it, Gatlin?"

"I mean it. I'll have to check in with the office every other day or so. Find someone to monitor my accounts while we're gone. I can't leave things unattended for a couple of weeks."

"A couple of weeks?" she says, stiffening. "You said two months, you promised me two months in the desert at a place of my choosing. That's what you said."

"Two months is too much, Sarah. I can't be gone that long. I can commit to one month. One month is the very best I can do."

Sarah brushes a lock of black hair off her forehead. She taps my bare chest with an index finger.

"A month is thirty-one days," she says, nodding her head. "That's thirty-one whole days in the desert. Start to finish."

"You've got yourself a deal."

"That's thirty-one days *in* the desert," she says, "not counting travel time there and back."

"All right, Sarah."

She claps her hands and rolls her body on top of mine. Sarah kisses me smack on the mouth.

It occurs to me that I might leave well enough alone, bask in the perfection of this moment and be content. Why don't I do that?

"And while we're clearing the air around here, Sarah, there's something else I want to tell you. Are you listening?"

"Yes," she says, taking a frisky bite of my ear.

"I've decided to visit the newborn at the hospital. His name is Jason."

Sarah lifts her head away from my face, then rolls off me onto her back. She pulls the sheet off the floor and under her chin.

"You said you were going to think about it," she says. "You said you weren't going to rush into anything."

"I have thought about it. I've been thinking about it since yesterday."

"You go up to that hospital," she says, studying the ceiling again, "and just as soon as you get to know that child, get close to him, he'll get sick and die. Maybe you think you can afford that. Maybe you've forgotten what can happen."

How to convince her otherwise?

"There was nothing anyone could have done about what happened, Sarah. There was nothing predestined or mysterious about our son's death. No one was being punished or singled out."

"I held that child in my arms," she says, showing me her empty, outstretched arms. "There wasn't a mark or a blemish on his entire body. He might have been sleeping, he might have opened his big eyes and looked right into mine. He was ours and he was perfect."

He was perfect, but he was not to be ours.

"You go tend to that child if that's what you feel you must do," she says. "I'm the smothering kiss of death."

"That's not true," I say, pulling her close to me. "You must not say that. Stop thinking it. Will you try? Will you promise me you'll try?"

"I won't have my heart broken again," she says.

"You cannot avoid life, Sarah. It's not a bad movie we can exit whenever we wish. It keeps coming."

"What do you want from me?" she says, sitting up in the bed.

"I want you to know it's surviving what happens that shapes us. That enduring changes, deepens our sense of what matters. And alters what remains."

"And love?" she says softly. "What happens when love changes? How do we get it back?"

She places her hand flat on my chest as if bracing herself for what follows.

"We begin by letting go. By accepting what's happened and going forward."

Sarah lays her cheek against the side of my arm but does not respond. After a pause, she runs a fingernail lightly down the center of my chest and stomach, circling my navel. My heart swells in its socket. Forgotten nerve cells flicker and twitch. Her hand is moving.

THE CLOCK on the bedside table reads 6:31 A.M. Sarah dozes beside me, perhaps dreaming of wide skies and open spaces. She sighs contentedly in her sleep, rolls onto her stomach and pulls the sheet over her head. In the grey pall of our bedroom I am reminded of some powerful sea creature sounding for air before plunging back into the vast dreamy deep. A single soft splash and then she's gone.

Above the bed, a white rectangular border of daylight now surrounds the westward-facing window. Outside something is stirring. A faint fluttering of wings. The world is waiting.

Birdy, birdy, birdy, birdy! Chip, chip, chip.

Coda

―――――――――――――――――――――

Saturday, October 23

 T HIS DAY finds me seated in the narrow stern of my new
canoe, the churning, brown Mississippi below, the swirling,
blue universe above. I am moving now, off about this mad
river business, on my way down to the Gulf. At my back a
rush of dry autumnal wind. The funky fish-and-mud smell of
the river, the surging action of the current, the world around
me rising and falling. Wind and wave. Just me and my reckless young friend, the haze on the horizon and the raging, big
river.

With each long stroke of his paddle, Matt creates a small
whirlpool on the river's surface and sends it spinning back
toward my end of the canoe. I place the flat blade of my
paddle into the brown water, making a whirlpool of my
own.

During the middle of the day we catch catfish in the

shaded pools along the bank. We leap out the side of the canoe and float on our backs in the cold running water beneath a wide, arching sky. We go ashore and hunt small game in the lush inland woods where big sycamores stand. Great piles of sculpted driftwood litter the earth. Overhead the dry leaves of the sycamores snap in the wind like paper pennants. A flock of blackbirds crashes from tree to tree. I sit quietly on the sand against a tree trunk, letting the light and sound wash over me.

With the coming of night we drag the canoe onto the head of a small island. We set up camp on the white sand alongside the murmuring current. Strange, gangly birds hoot from the thick foliage behind us. Fish jump. I throw myself out flat on my back on the dry sandbar and partake of my companion's trading tobacco. A ring of kindred spirits gathers by the fire.

Overhead ten million stars quiver and spin.

Out in the main channel of the river, her calliope bursting with song, her huge paddle wheel churning the brown water to chocolate foam, steams the Mississippi Queen. *She's traveling up river this clear October night, crawling slowly toward Baton Rouge and Vicksburg and beyond. She outshines the pumpkin moon.*

Just north of Plaquemine, on the flat sandbar of a small island, the steamboat's captain observes a great bonfire. In the glare of the firelight, two human figures stand silhouetted, their hands uplifted, their heads bowed before the Queen.